Over There

by
R. J. Reilly

© 2015 R. J. Reilly

All Rights Reserved.

No part of this publication may be reproduced, stored in a retrieval system, or transmitted, in any form or by any means, electronic, mechanical, photocopying, recording, or otherwise, without the written permission of the author.

First published by Dog Ear Publishing
4010 W. 86th Street, Ste H
Indianapolis, IN 46268
www.dogearpublishing.net

ISBN: 978-1-4575-3643-4

This book is printed on acid-free paper.

This book is a work of fiction. Places, events, and situations in this book are purely fictional and any resemblance to actual persons, living or dead, is coincidental.

Printed in the United States of America

Dedication

To my dear daughter, Mary Marguerite, and her family,
Dave, Margaret and Tim

Acknowledgements

Thanks to Jim McDonald, an early reader of this war story. And, as always, I wish to thank my daughters, Kathleen and Mary, and my granddaughter, Margaret, for their assistance with my book project, and Wendy Napiantek, for encouragement.

I was a GI in the last months of World War Two, so I lived through the time talked about in the book and by good fortune visited all the places described even though I had not heard of the Monuments Men or of the work they were doing. Reading Lynn H. Nicholas' *Rape of Europa: The Fate of Europe's Treasures in the Third Reich and the Second World War* (published in 1994) made me realize that even though I had visited the places described in my novel I had been, in reality, as ignorant as the narrator of this book and just as swept up in history. I am enormously indebted to Ms. Nicholas' book for many details.

Thanks to The U.S. National Archives & Records Administration for permission to use the photo on the cover, and thanks to Wikipedia, where I first saw it. The photo, dated April 24, 1945, shows German loot stored at Schlosskirche Ellingen in Bavaria, Germany, artwork found by troops of the U.S. Third Army. The image is a work of a U.S. Army soldier or employee, taken or made as part of that person's official duties. As a work of the U.S. federal government, the image is in the public domain. For more information about the photo: U.S. Department of Defense. Department of the Army. Office of the Chief Signal Officer - http://research.archives.gov/description/5757187.

Contents

Chapter 1

People in my generation still referred to World War Two simply as "The War," as if Korea and Vietnam and now Iraq and Afghanistan had not happened. But we didn't mean to denigrate those wars; a few of us foolish enough to join the reserves had even gone to Korea. It was just that after World War Two no other war seemed real to us, especially as we got older and Tom Brokaw told us we were the greatest generation, and Studs Terkel called our war "The Good War," and Bill Clinton, speaking at Normandy, told us we had saved the world. Most of us recognized the hyperbole, of course. Most of us hadn't really done much to save the world, but as the years passed we began to feel a kind of proprietary relationship to the war. Something that had been of great importance in our personal lives had also been important to the country and even to the world. And we had been there, we had been part of it. It was something that our children and grandchildren would never experience; it was one of the few mitigating elements in the generally ugly process of growing old.

But I hadn't thought of the war for a long time until the phone call. That had not only reminded me of the war, it had demanded that I think about it. The first part of the call had been short and to the point: was I the James Adair who had served with Lieutenant Alan West in Germany in 1945? When I said I was, there was a pause, and then the woman's voice said, "Well, finally. You wouldn't believe how many James Adairs there are in Michigan."

At first I thought she must be a telemarketer, but even a very clever telemarketer wouldn't have known about Lieutenant West, so I said, "Well, what can I do for you?"

"I'm Catherine Dunne, Lieutenant West's daughter," she said, "and I want to ask you some questions about my father. I hope you'll help. You're the only one who *can* help me."

I felt like a student who is asked a question he can't even understand, much less answer. "I haven't seen your father in sixty years," I said. "We never kept in touch. I don't even know where he is."

"He isn't anywhere," she said. "He's dead. He died two months ago, and he wasn't really anywhere for a long while before that. He had Alzheimer's."

That shocked me—not the fact that he was dead, because he was fifteen years older than I am, and that would make him in his nineties. The shock was the Alzheimer's. It seems to me that when certain special people disappear into that black hole it isn't just tragic. Earthquakes and famines and wars are tragic, but they kill people indiscriminately. But when Alzheimer's takes E. B. White or Alan West, you're reminded again that the world lacks a sense of what is appropriate. Certain minds shouldn't disintegrate, I felt; they should die cleanly and sharply, like people plunging off a high cliff. But I said the ritual things to the daughter about West's death—sorry for her loss, other generic phrases.

"I'm not really grieving," she said. "I didn't know him very well. That's why I tried to find you." She waited for a moment, but I didn't say anything, so she went on. "I suppose I sound dramatic, like someone on a soap serial. What seems important to me may be pretty pedestrian to you. People don't get excited about other people's family matters, do they? And it's a family matter I want to find out about." When I still didn't say anything—I was still thinking about the Alzheimer's—she said, "I don't want to impose. Am I keeping you from something? I could call later, or write, or even e-mail you if you have a computer."

I looked through the glass doorwall to the patio, where the impatiens and begonias were beginning to lose their color in the August heat. I had planted the flowers in hanging baskets, the way my wife had always done before she died. "You're not imposing," I said into the phone. "I have lots of time."

It was late afternoon when Catherine Dunne called and early evening before she had finished. Or not finished, really, just stopped. Once or twice her voice shook and she had to wait a moment, and several times she paused for so long that I thought the line had gone dead. It was indeed a family story she was trying to tell me, and it might well have been a plot for a soap serial if someone else had been telling it. But I suppose everyone's life is a soap serial when seen from the outside, and as she told it to me in fits and starts, with repetitions, and gobbets of irrelevant information about people who meant nothing to me, it was impossible not to be moved. Because if there was any coherence at all to her story it came from the part in her life that her father had played, or hadn't played, and as she talked I was remembering (also in fits and starts) her father as I had known him in the few months at the end of the war, the months she wanted so badly to know about, the months that she hoped would yield a kind of illumination for her, the months that had been something like that for me.

She had been only three when her father came home from Germany. He'd been gone most of her short life, first in the G-2 section of an infantry regiment unit, then (when I met him) in a newly formed Monuments, Fine Arts and Archives (MFAA) unit attached to the Seventh Army. The MFAA people were supposed to follow the troops into captured territory and take charge of any monuments or churches or artworks that had survived the war. When he came home—home was San Diego—she said, she had a father for the first time, but not for very long. He had taken a job as curator of a small private museum in Massachusetts, but she didn't understand then what that meant. She only knew he had to go away again and leave her because, for reasons that she didn't understand then, and didn't completely understand even now, her mother wouldn't go with him. "This didn't happen all at once," she said. "I suppose he was home for quite a while, and I suppose he and my mother must have talked over what they were going to do. Maybe they quarreled over it—I don't know. I only know that she and I were alone together again, and every once in a while my father would phone and I'd be put on the phone to talk to him and wouldn't know what to say."

She was in kindergarten when her mother remarried. "So I know there must have been a divorce, but it must have been quiet and uncomplicated, because I don't remember anything about it—don't remember my mother being upset or angry or anything at all." Then there was a stepfather, though she didn't think of him as that—she really didn't know what "stepfather" meant until the kids at school told her (a lot of them had stepfathers too). She grew to like him, but she was never really sure what her feelings toward him should be. She knew you were supposed to love your father, but she couldn't do that because she hardly ever saw him. Finally she decided to treat her stepfather like an uncle (she had two uncles on her mother's side), and just give up on the problem of how she should feel about her father.

Her father wrote her fairly frequently from Massachusetts—small talk, things about Boston he thought she might be interested in: the northeasters in the winter, the Revolutionary War sites (when she was older), sometimes the paintings or furniture or books that he dealt with. Once in a very great while her mother would put her on a non-stop flight to Boston for a visit. "But even then I knew the visits were duty visits," she said. "They were always hurried, even when both my father and I tried to pretend we were doing something natural." Once he had taken her up to Marblehead and they had gone out on a whale watch, her hat had blown away, and her father had bought her a new one with a Boston Red Sox logo on it. When she was eighteen and going to start college in California she had gone for a visit and he had taken her up to Maine, to Mount Desert Island on the coast, and at the top the onshore wind was so strong that you could lean against it like a building. "If I try to remember things that he said on those visits, I come up empty," she said, "except for that time in Maine at Mount Desert. I'd told him I'd be taking liberal arts courses, and he was pleased, and he said something about the value of the arts. I can't remember what it was exactly, some textbook thing, I thought at the time, something about unexpected help or companionship, but in my memory it seems to blur with leaning against the wind."

She was silent for a while after she'd said that, remembering, I suppose. Then she said, "I do remember now he said once that his favorite painters were the Dutch masters, and of course he had to explain who they were. He said they were his favorites among favorites." Then there were the college years, she said, and some college romances, and she always meant to go visit him, but somehow she never did, only wrote him occasionally. And then she'd gotten married to the last of the college beaus, and then there had been children, a girl and a boy, both in college in California now, and somewhere along the way she'd gotten divorced. In a way it was the divorce that had got her thinking about her father again. Her husband had been "unfaithful"; it seemed like such an old-fashioned term, but that was the case. And after he'd been gone for a while it occurred to her to wonder whether she was repeating her mother's life pattern. Her mother had never specifically said that her husband had been seeing another woman, but on the rare occasions that she'd ever referred to the matter to her daughter, she made it clear that she felt wronged. "Well, I feel wronged too," Catherine said. "I suppose every woman who gets divorced feels wronged, but it makes you wonder when you seem to be repeating something your parent has done, especially when you think you're very different from your parent."

At this point I had the feeling she'd been exposed to too much pop psychology, maybe from television analysts who always seemed to have a book they were flogging. But you can dismiss the TV analysts and their patients only if you don't know the patient at first hand. I was beginning to know the lieutenant's daughter, and I certainly had known her father, and whether or not she was lost in the labyrinth of pop psychology, her feelings didn't seem comical or insignificant to me. So once again I asked her the question which of course she couldn't answer. "What do you hope I can tell you about your father?"

"What he was like close up, day by day," she said. "You saw him in a way I never did. I saw his diary and his notebooks, and for five months you and one other person seemed to be with him all the time. I'd ask this other person about him too, if I could."

So she knew about Olivette as well as me. I was about to ask her how she'd happened to read his papers when she told me. A social worker from a Boston hospital—the Alzheimer unit—had written her because she was West's closest relative. The social worker thought someone might want to see the patient before the absolutely final stage. Catherine had phoned her mother with the news. "I suppose I thought she and I would go together," she said, "because it seemed like the proper thing to do. But she wouldn't go. She was sorry, she said, but for her it would be like visiting a stranger. She said, 'After all, they wrote to you, not me. But I don't think you should go either, unless you want to. He probably wouldn't know you anyway.' And she said something about Alzheimer wards being really ugly. Well, I went. I was alone anyway, the kids away at school, the husband long gone. Maybe my mother was right, that there wasn't really much point in going, but at the time there wasn't much point to anything else in my life either. Anyway, I went. And my mother was right. It was ugly."

It was ugly even before she got into the ward, she said. The door to the ward looked like a door in a prison—heavy metal, locked, a small window near the top with mesh across it. A phone in the wall next to the door had a sign telling visitors to call in and identify the patient they wanted to see. She did that, and after a few minutes an orderly came and let her in and told her that her father was in the day room and pointed her down a corridor. She didn't look into the rooms as she went down the corridor; she didn't want to see any more than she had to. The ward was scrupulously clean, she said, and even tried to be appealing, with pastel watercolors on the walls and the tile floor buffed and shining. But there was something wrong, she said, something about the air. It didn't smell bad exactly, but....I knew what she meant. I'd been to places like that. No matter what they did with fans and air fresheners there was always the faintest scent of aged bodies not wholly washed, the hint of excrement and old age. The day room was at the end of the corridor, and just as she got to the door a woman screamed somewhere behind her. "It was the kind of scream you hear in a horror movie," she said, "when a woman sees the zombie coming out of the closet or something. I looked around to see what was wrong, but there were two or three attendants in the hallway, and they weren't doing anything, so I guessed it was just business as usual, and I went into the day room." There was a large television in one corner. A quiz show of some kind was on, and three or four people were sitting on sofas in front of the set.

She looked around for her father, and the first man she saw was tall and lanky, like her father, but she could hardly look at his face because of what he was doing. He had on a hospital gown pulled up nearly to his waist, and as he sat watching the television he was massaging his penis with one hand and his testicles with the other. Her first reaction was to think that if that was her father she was going to turn around and leave, duty or no duty. But it wasn't her father. Her father was half sitting, half lying in a lounge chair near a window, but he wasn't looking out the window; he wasn't looking at anything. He was in pajamas and robe, but even from a distance she could see that he was almost skeletal. His hair was thin and white, and his face was hollowed and angular and longer than she remembered. "If I'd met him on the street I wouldn't have known him," she said, "and as soon as I thought that I started to cry. Because we'd lived all those years without seeing each other, and if he looked at me he probably wouldn't know me either. And I thought, What have we done with our lives?" But of course he didn't look at her, then or ever. They told her later that day that he had gradually stopped eating, that in the last day and a half he had had only sips of water. Did she want them to put in a feeding tube? "Translated," she said, "that meant, Do you want him to live comatose for a while, or do you want him to die? I wanted to tell them I hadn't seen him in twenty-five years and I didn't feel as if I had a right to decide whether he should live or die. But that wasn't their problem, of course. They let me think about it for a while. I sat and looked at my father. I even held his hand. I talked to him. But he never moved. Not even his eyes. You hear stories about people in comas being able to hear what people say to them, but I don't believe it. I didn't say goodbye or anything like that. It would have been play acting, because I was sure there wasn't anyone there."

So she stayed on till he died; it took two-and-a-half days. The hospital social worker who had called her in California told her that her father's apartment was still empty because he had had a yearly lease, and the social worker suggested that she stay there. She got her suitcase from the hotel when she left the hospital that day, took the train up to Lynn, identified herself to the landlord, and moved in. Her father's death two days later had been undramatic. It hadn't seemed to her that there was any difference in his appearance, but a nurse had said, "He's going now," and pressed the call button and a doctor and a Catholic hospital chaplain came in together. She told the priest her father wasn't Catholic, and the priest had simply nodded and asked if she would like her father to have conditional absolution. "I didn't really know what that was," she said, "but I guess I thought my father's dying was a solemn thing, and some kind of ritual seemed appropriate, and so he went ahead with it." The funeral had been perfunctory, a brief first step to cremation. The Catholic priest had agreed to say a few words, and then it was over. Two people from the museum were there, but they were only token mourners. Her father had retired several years before, and these people had barely known him.

But then, because she was next of kin and (as it turned out) heiress, there was a lawyer to be consulted and a will to be read. She received all her father's worldly possessions, which amounted to a very small bank account that barely covered funeral expenses, several shelves of books, a few paintings (mostly copies), and desk drawers stuffed with notebooks and odds and ends: old theater programs, exhibition notes, batches of what looked like old letters, score cards from old Red Sox games, and other things she hadn't bothered to look at yet. She had happened to look at some of the notebooks first, and it was there she'd found the references to me and to Olivette. She had called a packing company and had everything boxed up and shipped to California. When she got home she got the notebooks out and began to read them again, and it was then she decided to try to find me.

"So that's my story," she said. "I'm tired of talking, and I know you must be tired of listening."

I *had* been listening, of course, but it hadn't really seemed like listening. I hadn't had to prod myself to pay attention, because once I knew she was talking about Lieutenant West I kept seeing him, or trying to see him, as a father and husband and, finally, as Alzheimer victim, old, mindless, dead before he was dead. I kept trying to set the man I had known into the events I was hearing about, but it was an act of imagination I couldn't manage. So I said, "No, I'm not tired of listening." And I added, "I'll do what I can to help you, but I need some time to get my thoughts together."

"I'll give you my phone number," she said, "or I could even come to Michigan if you like."

I wrote down her phone number; a visit would have been too immediate. The older I got, the more I felt the complexity of most things, even things I thought I knew very well. I had thought I knew my wife very well, for instance, but now that she was gone I seemed to have discovered meanings in the way she had stood and layers of meaning in remarks she had made that I had been blind to when she was alive. I was rather like the old Puritan Jonathan Edwards, who thought he discovered new truths each time he read the same passage from the Bible. I was being asked now to return to and analyze a segment of my life that I hadn't understood at the time and hadn't thought about in fifty years. I really did need time to get my thoughts together. "I don't know what I'll have to say to you," I told her, "but I'll call you."

When I finally put the phone down my arm was stiff and the fingers had gone to sleep. I stood up and stretched and went out onto the patio and looked at the red impatiens and the yellow begonias. Most houses in southern Germany and Austria have flower boxes outside their windows filled with red geraniums, and in that spring of 1945, as it existed in my memory, all the houses in Austria and Bavaria were trimmed in scarlet like Christmas presents.

Chapter 2

In August, 1944, just two months after D-Day, American and French troops liberated Paris. I read about it in Camp Robinson, Arkansas, where our combat engineering battalion was still practicing blowing up barbed wire with Bangalore torpedoes and building pontoon bridges over Arkansas creeks. I read about it with the same sort of detachment that I read about the war in the Pacific. Both wars seemed very far away, and I saw myself as less a participant than a cheerleader. But in another two months we were on a Victory ship in New York harbor moving slowly past the Statue of Liberty on our way into the Atlantic. The Statue of Liberty made the war real to me; the lump in the throat and the racing heartbeat were a combination of homesickness and simple fear. Suddenly the war in the newspapers and on the radio and in the movies was my war too, and I knew I wasn't John Wayne, I was just a bookish nineteen-year old who was fond of quoting the easier poems of Byron, and I knew I would rather read about the war than be in it.

But England was comforting because we were overseas but not really in any danger. We lived in Quonset huts near an old private girls' school in Weston-super-Mare while we waited for our equipment to catch up with us; we bathed in the public baths; we drank lager and rough cider in the local pubs; and we went to the English equivalent of USO dances where a few old people with accordions and violins tried to play Benny Goodman jazz. I fell in love with England there: with the narrow streets, the tiny cars, the pubs with the odd names, the English accent and speech rhythms. It was all the way I'd seen it in the movies. I could almost imagine Rex Harrison leaping into a black Bentley and tearing off through the countryside in pursuit of Nazi spies. Once a week we drove to Bristol for supplies, and on the way back we sat in the bed of the six-by-six and ate chunks of bread still hot and soaked in butter.

But the German breakthrough in the Ardennes ended our English vacation, and I was reminded again of the real war. We moved out helterskelter, still without our heavy equipment, boarded a ship at Southampton, were violently seasick crossing the channel, and unsteadily debarked at Le Havre on New Year's morning, 1945. Since we had no trucks or jeeps, we walked for what seemed a very long way in a cold rain, then finally stopped and put up our pup tents. We wanted to borrow a piece of sheet metal from a local farmer to use for shelter, but none of us knew the French words either for "borrow" or for "roof." Next day we walked again, this time to railroad tracks, and we were loaded into a line of freight cars that looked small and boxy by American standards. Someone read the sign on the side of the cars and translated for us: forty men or eight horses. We didn't care: it was better than walking, and better than the boat ride across the channel. We stopped several times for piss call, and at one stop, I remember, outside a small station we saw a sign that said Paris de Bel-Air and guessed we must be going through the outskirts of Paris. Later we saw a sign with an arrow pointing to Rheims, then a sign for Bar-le-Duc, and someone with a map said, "We're heading dead east." He was right, and we kept going east till we got to Nancy, near Luneville, which at that time was the Seventh Army headquarters, and there we got off and waited for our equipment. We must have taken over some houses there, because I can remember being warm and having warm C-rations. We scraped our mess kits into big GI cans outside the mess tent, and children and sometimes grownups squabbled over the garbage. Odd, the tricks of memory. I remember the children at the garbage cans but not the house I lived in.

Then our equipment came and we moved out and we realized for the first time how cold it was. We heard afterwards that the 1945 winter was the coldest in a half century. All we knew at the time was that warmth was everything; we didn't think of sex or even of food, only warmth. In Luneville, at risk of court martial we snuck into the mess tent in order to lean for a moment against the Coleman stoves. Our dysentery drove us groaning into snow drifts to empty our watery bowels. When the unit moved it moved almost at walking speed. Trucks and flat bed trailers slid off the icy roads into ditches, and wreckers slid in after them. No one knew where we were, or cared. Years later, when I looked at some military history books and maps I could see that in those weeks we were a part of the Seventh Army's push east and south, from the Rhine toward Stuttgart and then Munich, but at the time our only reality was snow and ice and the occasional German planes that strafed us and added to our misery. We were green troops, most of us, working hard at staying alive those days. Later, when we learned the real dimensions of the German attack, we could only marvel that they had not only stayed alive but had moved thousands of infantry and hundreds of tanks through the Ardennes in the same weather we found unbearable, and had fought us to a standstill. I remember thinking that if they had been Americans we would have attributed their bravery to their patriotic and political beliefs; we would have seen their attack as evidence of the power of democratic ideals. But they were Nazis, some of them SS troops, motivated (we believed) by the worst sort of beliefs. I puzzled over the problem for a day or so, not realizing at the time that I hadn't yet shed my movie notions about war.

Chapter 3

The bitter weather began to ease up in late March. We had crossed the Rhine at Karlsruhe and had got to the Neckar River near Heilbronn. It was in Heilbronn that I first saw Lieutenant West and Olivette Normandin. The town had been secured only the day before by the 100th Infantry Division. A corporal from that division told me that it had been a bad several days, and that on the last day a bunch of Hitler Jugend boys had come running out of a factory to surrender. They were crying, he said, and their officers were trying to shoot them. Just kids, he said, some of them only thirteen years old. "He caught them young and brainwashed them," the corporal said, and at the time I didn't say anything, though I thought again, What if they were American boys fighting an enemy—would we say they were brainwashed?

Heilbronn was pretty badly shot up. Our temporary battalion HQ was in an old factory building with all the windows shot out and the main door hanging crookedly on its hinges. Parked in front of the building was an old black Renault, apparently once a French taxi since it had fare prices marked on the door. It looked old and battered and decrepit enough to have been one of the original taxis of the Marne twenty-five years before. A tall, lanky man in officer's ODs was standing next to it talking to our battalion commander, and I could just make out a dark haired woman in the front passenger seat. The man was wearing lieutenant's bars, but what struck me as odd was that he wasn't carrying any side arms. That night someone said they were from the "arty outfit," and that he'd heard they were going to be traveling with us. When someone else asked what the arty outfit was, a sergeant from headquarters said, "MFAA," and when no one could guess what the acronym meant, he finally told them. And then I remembered a sign I'd seen outside a bombed-out church—I think it was in Bitche—with the initials MFAA. The sign had said the church was off limits to military personnel by order of the Supreme Commander. The Supreme Commander was General Eisenhower, of course, and so the sign clearly meant business, but I didn't know why at the time.

Then it was late in April, and we all knew the war was almost over. We listened to Armed Forces Radio and read *Stars and Stripes*, but we knew the end was coming from other things as well. The DPs (the displaced persons) were moving in droves like cattle let out of their pens. They clogged the main road between Heilbronn and Mannheim, they swarmed around our cooking tents and mess halls, they begged and stole from us, from the Germans and from each other. They were always in the way, pathetic in their wooden clogs and miscellaneous scraps of clothes. We hadn't done anything to them, yet they made us feel guilty, because we had never before seen people who had absolutely nothing. We felt rich and bloated when we looked at them, so we gave them C-rations and candy bars and got away from them as fast as we could. The houses along the Neckar River, in Heilbronn, Neckarsulm, and Heidelberg began to show white bed sheets in their windows, flags of surrender. Elderly German men and women stepped politely aside when we met them in the street. Children peeked at us from windows and doorways. Everyone knew the war was nearly over, and we were conquerors. We felt something we had never felt before, the sense of absolute power, the awareness of being feared, the strange tonic of being fawned on and toadied to. I remember feeling frightened at this sense of dominance, and because I was nineteen this awareness of dominance took mostly a sexual form, and my daydreams and night dreams were full of scenes in which German girls, frightened or sullen or stubborn, yielded to my passion. But, as I saw now, even in the most detailed and erotic of those scenes, when the orgy was over the German girls always realized that our affair was not just a sexual encounter but something more. What the something more was wasn't clear in the dreams, but both the German girl of the moment and I knew that what we had just done was at least "not just." As the twig is bent, so grows the tree, of course; I'd left parochial school, but parochial school hadn't left me.

It was in Neckarsulm that I finally met Lieutenant West and Olivette Normandin. I knew they had been traveling with us, and I had caught a glimpse now and then of the old Renault on the river road, always trailing black exhaust fumes. Neckarsulm seemed to be our last stop, though no one said that officially. The cooks commandeered a building instead of setting up the mess tent, and the officers took over a block of flats on the west side of the river. We all took these moves as signs of permanence. I was changing a tire on my truck when our first sergeant told me I was wanted at headquarters. That sounded ominous. PFCs aren't called to headquarters for social reasons, and the company captain was no one's favorite. Enlisted men have an inherent dislike of officers, of course, based on the old caste system that still implies that enlisted men are social inferiors to their officers. But officers are also gossiped about, and the gossip—some of it true, much of it imagined—sets the officers' character for the enlisted men. We had long ago pegged our captain as an ersatz John Wayne. He'd told someone that he wished we'd had more combat, that he didn't feel we had done as much as we could have done. But we also knew that he had been a meter reader for a gas company in civilian life and that he'd got his commission by being in the National Guard, not the regular army. So we disliked him for pretending to be more than a civilian soldier, like the rest of us.

When I had saluted and given my name and he had put me at ease, he said, "I've got a special detail for you because they tell me you're the arty type." I didn't know where he'd got that notion, but it was clear he didn't mean it as a compliment. "You're going to be driver for Lieutenant West and his lady friend till further notice. Their car has gone kaput and they've asked for a jeep. But we have no jeeps available, and no three-quarter tons, only six-bys, and since they can't drive six-bys you're their driver. So go look them up and introduce yourself."

I said, "Yes, sir."

"I dislike this detail because it has nothing to do with the war," he said, "but I'm a soldier and I follow orders. But if we weren't so close to finishing this thing—" He stopped, remembering, I suppose, that he was talking to a PFC. I knew what he meant, though. John Wayne wouldn't have his people chasing around after paintings and monuments; they'd be going hell for leather after the enemy. "Anyway," he said, "you're to follow Lieutenant West's orders, unless the Nazis surprise us again, and then you hightail it back to the outfit." I thought he brightened a little at the thought of another Ardennes, but only for a moment. Then he said brusquely, "You're not to regard this detail as a vacation. Remember you're a soldier and that this is dangerous country, war or no war."

I said, "Yes, sir" again and saluted and went out.

They had given West and Olivette Normandin a first floor unit in a block of flats near the town square. I didn't know if there was a protocol for an enlisted man calling on an officer, so I simply knocked on the front door and waited. Olivette Normandin opened it, and I saw her up close for the first time. She was wearing a uniform that seemed to be part American and part something else, French, I supposed. The trousers were some sort of dark blue twill, her shirt looked like a GI suntan issue, and over that she wore an Eisenhower jacket, unbuttoned. She was short and slight, not much more than five feet tall, had a sallow complexion and very dark hair and eyes, and (I thought) could be Greek or Italian. When I told her who I was she put out her hand for a formal handshake, a gesture of civility so unexpected that I almost didn't respond.

"Come into the kitchen," she said. "Lieutenant West will want to meet you." Her English was unforced, with just a touch of something foreign that I couldn't identify at the time.

I followed her down a short hallway and into a small kitchen at the rear of the flat. West was sitting at a tile-topped table that was crowded with maps and wine glasses and a tall bottle of white wine. He was smoking a cigarette in a rather long cigarette holder, the kind I hadn't ever seen except in movies with aristocratic foreigners in full dinner dress. It was the first of many signs that he was a being outside my usual world.

"This is First Class Private Adair," Olivette Normandin said. "He's to be our driver."

I didn't know whether to salute, and while I was trying to decide, West stood up and came over and put his hand out and we shook hands. He was probably six-feet three or four and lanky, so that he looked even taller. He had brown hair that stood up in a brush in front and the kind of light blue eyes that are almost gray. "I suppose you'd like to know something about the outfit you're getting into," he said, "so take a seat and we'll have a chat." He went back to his seat at the table and gestured for me to sit across from him. I'd left my helmet in the truck, but I was still wearing the helmet liner, so I tucked that under my chair and tried to look comfortable.

"We're tasting some German wine," he said, "and finding it not worth going to war for, but it's better than nothing. Try some while we tell you what we do." He filled a squat water glass and handed it to me.

Like everyone else in my company I had drunk wine and calvados and whatever else had come my way in France and Germany. We had no taste, of course; whatever made us drunk would do. But I sipped the wine and pretended to savor it.

And then West began to talk. Olivette Normandin had sat down at the table now and had taken a glass of wine, and though she seemed to be listening to West, I had the feeling that she was looking me over, taking my measure, and I felt scruffy and unkempt. And in a few minutes I also felt something else: a sense that I was hopelessly out of my depth. West was describing what the MFAA people were doing in the war, and I know now, remembering the drift of his talk, though not the exact words, that he was taking pains not to talk over my head. But he was failing, not because he wasn't trying, but because I was so invincibly ignorant. For me, the war meant being cold and hungry and afraid; my personal contacts with war were with simple and concrete things: M-30 carbines, GMC six-by-sixes, C-rations, dysentery. And on the enemy side, more concrete things: Messerschmitts, 88's, burnt-out Tiger tanks, wood-burning trucks, the ruins of Mannheim. But the world of war that West described, with Olivette nodding agreement, was not my limited world. In my increasingly muzzy mind, I seemed to catch glimpses of a higher and better world than mine, one that was dangerous and unpleasant, like mine, but one that had some meaning, some significance, some reference to futurity that mine lacked. People in their world scrambled to stay alive, as I did in mine, but their staying alive had more than personal importance. The glimpses I had didn't form a coherent vision, only a vague sense that they and people like them were saving the world through art.

The more wine I sipped, the more some of the names they mentioned began to ring in my mind like poetry: Rembrandt, *The Madonna of the Rocks*, Raphael, *The Adoration of the Lamb*. Olivette Normandin told me the story of Rose Valland, whom she called the lady of the something or other (which West translated as "tennis court"). Rose Valland had been curator of the museum in Paris where the Nazis deposited much of their stolen paintings, sculptures, jewelry and furniture, and for four years she had kept secret records of what arrived there and where it was to be hidden—in salt mines in Austria and castles and monasteries all over Bavaria. If the Gestapo had caught her, it would have meant death, likely a slow death. Olivette and West were following some of those leads now, tracking down artworks intended for Goering's mansion or Hitler's museum in Linz.

"They stole the manifestations of our soul," Olivette said, "and we want them back."

"Olivette has left out a few things," West said. "She helped Rose Valland make some of the copies of those records, for one thing."

Olivette shrugged. "That was only a secondary danger," she said, "hardly more than just being alive in Paris under the Germans. Rose was the one who really dared."

I remembered a scene in a war movie in which Rex Harrison drove his Bentley through a border barricade and eluded the Nazis, and I thought, That was movie bravery, all fast action, everything over in a moment, but what Rose Valland had done was slow and would be hard to dramatize, and she had to be brave every day for four years. In my mind I saw the museum as old and huge, a vague expanse of high ceilinged rooms, all filled with paintings stacked against the walls, with Nazi guards in field gray and polished boots patrolling the corridors, and Rose Valland in some dark basement room, writing titles and names of places by candle light, always hearing footsteps, waiting for the door to burst open. I hadn't ever been brave in the war, I reflected, only scared and sick. I knew all about the Gestapo from the movies, of course, and I couldn't imagine myself doing what Rose Valland had done. And that made me wonder again about what had driven her to take those risks: to save works of art. West and Olivette thought her bravery was remarkable, but not her motivation. So they knew something that I did not; they were in touch with something that I knew nothing about. I sat and took in their quiet air of matter of factness about art and the people who risked their lives to protect it, and I felt a gulf between them and me; I wanted desperately to be knowledgeable, like them; I wanted to understand the kind of life that had art as its core. I felt shabby and small, an outsider so ignorant he could only guess at what he was missing. And then, with the wine working on me even more, I thought of Olivette's phrase, art as the manifestation of the soul. I was young and not quite sober; I felt the words almost like an incantation, and though I was vague about its meaning, I knew I wanted to be able to make sentences like that and to believe what those sentences said.

When I left them that day my head was heavy with wine and vague aspiration. Our company had taken over a block of buildings that included three or four small stores, a machine shop, and a tavern. The officers took over the tavern, of course, and the rest of us were spread out in the other buildings. There were no real bathrooms, but there was running water, and we found some tubs and half barrels that we could fill up for washing and shaving. West and Olivette Normandin had been only casually dressed, though my imagination painted them as more civilized than I, but that next day the only improvement I could improvise was to be neater and cleaner than I had been the day before. When I reported, they were seated at the kitchen table again, with the maps still on the table but with coffee cups and cans of C-ration scrambled eggs in place of wine glasses. They had found a coffee pot somewhere, and Olivette poured a cup for me.

"We're going to make a run back to Heilbronn today," West said. "There are salt mines there that we think are full of stuff, some of it really big stuff according to rumor. At least one Rembrandt, and maybe the stained glass windows from the Strasbourg cathedral, and books, lots of books, maybe the whole Heidelberg University library."

I couldn't take in what he was saying. "Why are those things there?" I said, "and why in a salt mine?"

"Salt mines are deep," he said, "good bomb shelters." He pushed a map over in front of me, a fairly large scale map of western Europe, with France and Germany colored red. "The Germans didn't retreat when we started to bomb, first in France, then in Germany, but their treasures retreated. As the bombing moved east, most of what they'd looted was sent east for safety. Truck loads. Whole train loads. Look at the map. From Paris and Rheims east to Cologne and Frankfurt, then east to Berlin and Leipzig, running away from the bombing. Now look down here." He ran his finger southwest from Wurzburg to Stuttgart, to Augsburg, to Munich. "All through this southwestern area are salt mines, hundreds of feet deep, safe from bombs and perfect for storage of artworks. Temperature always about 55 degrees, humidity about 65 percent—cool, dry air, the sort that keeps mummies from rotting. That's where the Rembrandts went, and the Vermeers, and the Raphaels, and a lot of their own things too, from museums and libraries—to the salt mines and probably to some schlosses down there in the same area. We think the whole world down there is like treasure island."

"It's also where they say Hitler is going to make his last stand," Olivette said. "You know, of course, that he ordered Paris to be burned when the Germans left. I believe if he gets to Bavaria he will take all the artworks with him when he dies."

As I think back to that conversation now, sixty years later, I realize that it must have taken place at the end of April, and that Hitler was probably dead, but of course we didn't know that. We knew—or thought we knew—that the Russians were in Berlin, but no one knew anything about Hitler. In the weeks that followed we heard all sorts of things about him: that he was dead, that he'd flown out of Berlin just before the Russians got there and was in South America, that he was somewhere near where we were, in Bavaria or western Austria, in disguise, sometimes as a DP, sometimes as a priest, sometimes even as an American officer. We felt the power of the growing myth. We found ourselves looking critically at German men of medium height with eyes of a certain intensity. He'd lost the war and his country was in ruins, and we supposed he was only a refugee on the run, and yet the thought that we might see his face for a moment in a crowd was unsettling, as if, like Dracula, he might be immune to ordinary death. Much later, when everyone saw pictures of the burned bodies, the Russians were still not convinced he was dead. I remember West saying that the Russians were right in the spirit, if not the letter. "I think he may be dead all right," he said, "but he didn't take the Nazi mind with him." And Olivette Normandin was right about Hitler wanting to take the hidden artworks with him. We didn't get into the Heilbronn mines that day because the American bombing had knocked out all the power there. Water from the Neckar River had seeped into the mine, and the pumps that usually ran were under water. West heard from another MFAA man later that the mine had been wired to blow up before the Americans got there, but for some reason that hadn't happened, and that the Rembrandt and the Strasbourg cathedral window panes and thousands of other things were safe.

"Vengeance even after death," Olivette said to us. "But I wish to be fair. It was a German general who refused to destroy Paris in spite of Hitler's orders. So that says something about the German mind. But on the other hand, no Frenchman would ever order artworks to be destroyed, for whatever reason. That says something about the French mind."

West said nothing about Olivette's comment, and of course I didn't either. But next day I was changing a tire on my truck and West came down to the motor pool to see when we could leave. I was taking a break, sitting on the running board. Changing a tire meant taking the wheel off and pounding on the tire with a sledge hammer to get the tube off the rim. I started to get up, not sure where West stood on the saluting protocol, but he motioned me back to the running board and sat down on the fender of a three-quarter ton next to my truck, like a man settling down for a chat, but I'd never had a chat with an officer before.

"I notice your truck's bare," he said. He meant that there was no tarpaulin covering the bed.

"I've got the tarp and the hoops," I said. I'd taken them off a week or two before when we had to carry some French DPs from a work camp in Passau back to a depot near Mannheim. I told him about the trip: the bed of the truck jammed with people, most of them middle-aged or older, standing up shoulder to shoulder, yelling insults I couldn't understand at any Germans we passed. Someone had made a French flag out of an old bed sheet, and the tricolor billowed above the truck like a sail. Two old women were stuffed into the truck cab with me, and every time I had to shift gears I banged the knee of the old lady next to me, and I kept saying, "Pardon, Madame," in my best French. She never took her eyes off the rosary she had laced over her fingers. "I don't know why they were in a work camp," I said. "They looked too old to work. But it was exciting. I wish I could have talked to them."

West listened, though he wasn't looking at me. I'd already discovered that he often looked away from people when he was listening or talking himself, as if not to be distracted. "We're in chaos now," he said. "Everything's broken down. Anything can happen. Maybe there was an order to dispose of those people and it got mislaid. Or maybe they made themselves useful cleaning latrines. Or maybe someone in charge just didn't want to kill them."

"Like the German general in Paris," I said.

"Yes, there must be many like that," he said, "though it's hard for Mme. Normandin to admit that."

I said, "I was thinking about what she said, about Hitler wanting to destroy paintings and books and things, and how no Frenchman would ever do that."

West looked off into space again. "You and I, Jimmy, can't guess what it was like to be under the German occupation for four years. It must have been like being in jail for four years, and I suppose all prisoners hate their jailers. You and I know there are good Germans, kind Germans, great German artists—Bach and Beethoven and Goethe and all the rest. So does she. But that's not what she saw in Paris for four years. I suppose she feels what those French people in your truck feel—that they're different from the Germans, and better. That's national feeling, patriotism, whatever you want to call it. It's why we have wars."

I didn't know what to make of that, whether he was explaining Olivette's feelings or blaming her for them. "I guess I'd have felt the same way if I were French," I said.

"Sure, so would I," he said. "We're patriots too. We don't talk much about it, but we're proud that the USA went to war to stop Hitler, aren't we?"

"Sure," I said. I'd wanted to go, had been afraid they'd find something wrong and make me 4-F.

"Most of the people in this war are patriots," he said, "except maybe the DPs, those people who didn't have a dog in this fight but got dragged into it. We're patriots fighting patriots."

I thought of the hill outside of Luneville I'd seen in February. Snow two-feet deep, a few splintered trees, lumps here and there in the snow, patches of olive drab. The lumps were frozen GIs waiting for the Graves Registration people to pick them up before the spring thaw. It occurred to me now that there were probably patches of gray too; I didn't know what the Graves people did with enemy bodies. "I've always thought the Germans were bamboozled by Hitler," I said, "like the Hitler youth kids."

"I'm sure they were," West said, "but they were only bamboozled because they loved their country. If they hadn't identified themselves with Germany they wouldn't have listened to Hitler."

"You make it sound as if patriotism's a bad thing," I said.

"Not a bad thing, only a natural thing," he said. "You love your family, you come to have a feeling for your neighborhood, then your city, and state, and then whole country—like the stone dropped in the pond sending out ripples. It'd be unnatural if we didn't feel these things. But it's a dangerous thing."

"Then—"

But he broke in. "I only mean it's these feelings that make us angry enough to fight," he said.

I was nineteen, and the notion that the Hitler youths and I were much alike upset me. "But we're right, aren't we? I mean, we're right and the Nazis are wrong."

"Oh, sure," he said, "or at least we're more right than they are. I hope we can stay that way."

I didn't ask him what he meant by that. I picked up my sledge hammer and went at the tire rim again. But I was thinking of the way you feel at a ball game when they play "The Star Spangled Banner." You think it's kind of corny, and you may be too embarrassed to sing, but you feel something that you think is good. But that only made me think that the Germans probably had a national anthem too and had the same kind of feeling when they heard it.

West came over and put his foot on the tire to keep it from jumping away from me when I pounded it. "When you go back home and go to college, Jimmy," he said, "you'll hear what I've been saying in your first course in sociology or psychology. It'll be called something like 'National Mores and Beliefs.'"

It was the second time he'd called me "Jimmy," and each time I'd felt a little lift of spirit, as if just calling me by name he had somehow given me special recognition. I was sure I'd never be on a first name basis with him, though. I had argued with him a little bit a moment before, but that had been like being called on by the teacher in a class room discussion. You could give an opinion, but you wouldn't call the teacher by his first name. I suppose that was how I really saw West in those days, as a teacher, but not as an ordinary one. In later years I had many teachers, some of them remarkable, but none who had what stage people call the "presence" that West had. He didn't seem to be a person talking about a subject; he seemed somehow to be part of it, to be talking from the inside. When he talked about Rembrandt's self-portraits one night a week or two later I could almost feel with Rembrandt the problems of painting from a mirror image. It was a subject that I suppose an art historian could lecture on, but West wasn't lecturing; he was talking casually, the way a professional ball player might talk to a friend in a bar about how to hit a curve ball.

I got the tube loose and began to patch it. And then it occurred to me that he'd referred to Olivette Normandin as Madame Normandin, and I knew enough French to know that "Madame" meant "Mrs." I knew that she and West were living in the same apartment, and I knew that they'd been traveling together. In those end-of-the-war days some of our officers had German women or DP women living with them. We hated them for it not on moral grounds but because it was a privilege of rank, and so we always used the slang term and said they were shacking up. But now I didn't want to think of West and Olivette Normandin as just shacking up, especially if Olivette was married. Since I censored even my own sexual dreams, I suppose it wasn't surprising that I wanted to censor their lives as well. The bent twig phenomenon again.

I finished putting the wheel back together again and leaned it against the running board.

"You carry a tire pump?" West asked me.

"I don't have one," I said. "I take my flats to the motor pool. They have a compressor."

"I'm asking because we've got a long run tomorrow," West said, "with lots of places for flat tires."

"I can run on only three wheels if I don't have a load." I had double axles on the rear, with dual tires on each axle. I could run without the outside duals if I had to.

"We won't have any load on the way down and probably not on the way back either," West said. "We've had word about a place down south packed with stuff. It's a long way and no easy way to get there." He took a folded map from his shirt pocket and spread it out on the hood of the truck. It wasn't an army map; it looked more like the kind of map you get from AAA. He pointed to Neckarsulm and then slid his finger south and a bit east to a name on the border of Austria: Fussen. I could see at a glance there was no direct way to get there. West moved his finger over thin dotted lines—secondary roads. East to Schwabisch Hall, across the Danube to Augsburg, then south along the Lech River to Fussen. "Thank the army," West said, "you get to see some of the Alps. And I don't think you'll forget Neuschwanstein."

Next morning I got out my shelter half and blanket and mess kit and put them in the back of my truck along with my tarp and hoops because it looked as if we'd be staying overnight somewhere down there.

I'd thought about the Alps before I went to sleep the night before, or tried to think about them. But all I could conjure up was a hazy picture of mountains I'd seen in movies, and I wasn't sure they were even the right mountains.

West and Olivette Normandin were waiting for me when I got to their apartment. West stood up on the running board and dropped their bags next to mine in the truck, and they climbed into the cab, Olivette in the middle next to me. It seemed to me I caught a whiff of scent, but I couldn't be sure I wasn't imagining it, like the touches of romance in my erotic dreams. If it was real, it was gone in a minute because my truck had a canvas top but no doors, and as soon as we were rolling we had a breeze.

"This is like riding in an old-fashioned carriage," Olivette said, "as if we were going on a picnic somewhere."

What she said echoed what I was thinking; I felt as if I were skipping school on this excursion. I was leaving army drabness and routine behind and going to the Alps, the mountains of everyone's imagination. And though I was only a truck driver I was a vital instrument: I was taking important people to a place where they would do important things. I think I had some vague notion that West and Olivette would disappear down a salt mine and come up carrying paintings and statues of enormous value, and that they would load these things in my truck and we would deliver them somewhere. Newsreel cameras might even be there to record our exploits.

The road west to Schwabisch Hall was the usual bad secondary road. It hadn't been broken up by bombing or artillery, but it had never been built to withstand tank and heavy equipment traffic. It was crumbling and rutted, reinforcement rods and wires stuck up out of the concrete, and we couldn't make much speed. But things picked up when we got to Augsburg. We went up a long gentle hill into the city, and at the crest of the hill was a gigantic banner slung between trees: "The U.S. 7th Army Welcomes You To Augsburg." And then finally there was a decent road south along a river that the map said was the Lech River, and we barreled along at 60 mph. We were getting into the Alps now. The uphill grades were getting steeper, and in the distance we could see mountains that looked so high and so massive they took my breath away. It was late afternoon, but the May sun was still high in the sky. All the colors seemed pure and startling: the valley greens, the white of the snow caps, the intense blue of the background sky. I had to pull off the road and simply stare for a few minutes.

West and Olivette seemed to understand. "The first time is almost too much, isn't it?" West said. He offered a canteen of wine to Olivette, and when she'd taken a drink she gave it to me. I drank some, but I could hardly taste it, as if all my senses were concentrated on the mountains.

Olivette said, "If they were fighting just for this you could understand."

I said, "Do you think the Germans are still holed up down here?" We'd heard a lot about the Southern Redoubt where the Germans were supposed to make a last stand.

"Maybe some," West said. "There may be some who haven't heard Hitler's dead. And maybe some who'll fight anyway."

"Out of spite," Olivette said.

"I guess that's as good a word as any," West said.

"Are we anywhere near Berchtesgaden?" I asked.

West spread the map out on Olivette's lap, and we all looked at it. I could see Fussen on the Austrian border, and east of it, maybe thirty miles, I guessed, was Berchtesgaden. Even with the Alps around me the name seemed somehow imaginary, though really that whole trip down seemed pleasantly imaginary to me, with Olivette next to me and West telling us stories about mad King Ludwig and his fairy tale castles—Neuschwanstein and Herrenchiemsee—and the wine from the canteen, and then the incredible panorama of the Alps.

"I've read that they killed King Ludwig so he couldn't build any more castles," Olivette said, "because he was bankrupting Bavaria. I've also read that they killed him because he loved Wagner."

"It seems a bit extreme either way," West said. I guessed they were joking, but the joke went by me, and in a moment I knew that West sensed this, because for the next few minutes he told funny stories about Ludwig and his castles, and added that it was ironic that Hitler liked the music that had got Ludwig killed—even if that story was a joke. I knew the stories were for my benefit, and I hoped that wasn't obvious to Olivette. I made a mental note to look up something about Wagner ("Vogner," they called him) when I had a chance.

From all that West had said about the Neuschwanstein castle I should have been prepared when I finally saw it, but I wasn't. We had come around a bend and seemed to be heading for a wall of solid pine trees when the road bent again and the pines parted like a curtain and there was the castle perched on a mountain side like a gigantic Christmas ornament. It really did look like a gingerbread castle; I couldn't imagine the delicate spires and towers made out of anything solid. Before I could read, my mother had read me some of the Grimm fairy tales and showed me some of the illustrations, and all I could think of now was that the castle looked something like the one where the princess let down her hair for her lover. As we made another turn we could see the placid lake behind the castle, the one, I supposed, where Ludwig was drowned. "It looks like a movie castle," I said, and forty years later I remembered that remark when I took my grandchildren to Disneyland. I wanted to tell them that the Disney castle was only make-believe and that I had been to the real one, but when I thought about it I had to admit that Ludwig's castle was make-believe too. They were both false but for different reasons: Disney's imitation was meant to make money; Ludwig's imitation was meant to provide a setting for Wagner's romanticizing of medieval German history. I had learned by then to pronounce Wagner's name and to prefer Bach and Mozart to Wagner, but as I watched Mickey Mouse and Donald Duck lead the parade to the castle, I knew I preferred mad Ludwig's intention.

We went down a long twisting grade that brought us to level ground at the foot of the mountain, and as we looked upward we could see the giant entrance way to the castle. There were several jeeps and a few weapons carriers parked, mostly Seventh Army, two or three with Third Army markings. Two GIs with carbines stood at the foot of the long stone staircase up to the entrance. West got out and went over to the GIs, then came back to the truck. "Some of our people are up there," he said. "I've got ID for Mme. Normandin and me, but they're being very tough about regular army people going in. I guess you'll have to see the place from the outside, Jimmy."

So for the next couple of hours I joined other GI drivers in staring up at the castle. This close, it was even more incredible, because now I could see the smaller refinements of ornamentation, but still the strongest impression it gave was that of an exotic organism, some strange plant or fungus springing upward; the spires at different heights looked like irregular growths from a main trunk, and the out buildings, smaller towers, looked like droppings from the trunk that had taken root.

I sat for a while with Miller, a T-5 from Cleveland who'd driven some Third Army people. "Doesn't look much like a warehouse, does it?" he said, "but they say it's stuffed to the rafters. Statues, paintings, furniture, carpets, you name it. Loot. My captain says there's one room with so many carpets that it's like walking on a mattress."

"What are they going to do with it?" I said.

He shrugged. "Take it someplace. No one seems to know where though."

"They'll have to give all that stuff back to the owners," I said.

"I suppose," he said. "Hell of a job though." And then he added, "I'd say a lot of people will make a lot of money out of this stuff, one way or another. They won't let us GIs in—afraid we'd steal something. Officers don't steal, though, do they?"

"No," I said, "everyone knows that."

A figure appeared at the top of the steps to the castle and started down. When it was halfway down I could see that it was Olivette. When it was clear that she was coming toward us Miller said, "Who's the tootsie?"

"She's a French lady, helping out my Monuments man."

When she was just out of earshot Miller said, "Oo la la."

"Not Oo la la," I said, "she's an art expert."

"Well, so am I," he said, "Oo la la."

He stayed for a moment when Olivette came up, but when I didn't introduce him he went back toward his jeep.

Olivette said, "They're talking about logistics in there. That's a word that's not in my English dictionary, but apparently it has to do with trucks and so forth, and I can't be of any help with that. So I thought I'd come down and keep you company."

I groped for something casual to say but came up with nothing. I'd only been with her in West's company, and I wasn't sure of my status. Over her shoulder I could see Miller mouthing the words "Oo la la," and that made me even edgier. Finally I said, "Someone down the line's got some coffee. Can I get you some?"

I was sure she felt my awkwardness—I've often thought social ineptness gives off signals of some kind—but she merely said, "That would be marvelous," and sat down on the front bumper.

I brought the coffee back in our canteen cups, and we sat down on the bumper. I'd told Miller she was a lady. I didn't know how else to describe her. I hadn't got over the feeling I had when I met her and West: that they were "older" than I, by which I meant that by my nineteen-year old standards they were middle-aged, not terribly old like my parents, but significantly older than people like Miller and me, and therefore different. Now, as I looked sideways at her, I felt that category slipping away. She had opened her Ike jacket, and I could see the push of her breasts under the suntan shirt, and I was sure now that I caught a scent of perfume. Because I had dismissed her from my world, I hadn't ever really looked at her. I had known she was small and dark eyed, but no more than that. Now quite suddenly I was aware of the shape of her nose and the way her hair came to a widow's peak on her forehead, and the fact that her hands on the canteen cup showed short fingernails without polish.

I said, "What did you find in there?"

She said, "What we thought we'd find, but it's still hard to believe. We found what Rose said we'd find—hundreds of things stamped ERR," and she said something in German that I couldn't follow. She took a piece of notepaper from her pocket and printed it out for me: ERR: *Einsatzstab Reischleiter Rosenberg*, which meant, roughly, "Rosenberg's project." Rosenberg was Hitler's chosen art collector, she said, the man who selected which looted artworks would be set aside for the art museum that Hitler was going to build in Linz. Rose Valland, checking her secret records, had told them that they would find a huge cache of things stamped ERR at Neuschwanstein and further east at a mine called Altaussee. "And, yes, we found them," she said again, and she told me how she and West and the others had gone up the spiral staircases from one level to another, finding paintings by the hundreds, tapestries, even chests containing what she called "the famous Rothschild jewels." They had found Rosenberg's photographic laboratory, where all the items were photographed, and even filing cases with catalogues for all the private collections that had been stolen, so that now restoring them to their owners would be possible. She put down her cup. "I love art," she said.

"It is not too much to say that I live for art. But today was too much. The Germans stole art in bulk; they stole by artists' names, I think, not by quality or personal liking. Today I feel as if I have been looking at rooms full of money, like gold bullion."

"I wish I could have gone in," I said. "I wish I could have seen some of those things. I wouldn't have known good from bad though."

"Don't feel bad," she said. "Most people wouldn't. Taste in art isn't a natural thing, like an ear for music or good eyesight. You have to acquire it."

"But how?"

"How do you learn anything? You study it."

"You mean in school?"

"Maybe in school, maybe other ways. Maybe looking and looking at paintings, maybe reading about them, finding out when they were made, what the painter or sculptor thought he was doing and why. It's work, it consumes time, so you have to be interested to begin with, not just snobbish, wanting to impress people."

For a moment I thought she meant me, because as soon as she said it I thought, "Why do I want to be like them, talk like them, when I've never looked at paintings, maybe never will?" But of course she wasn't thinking of me; she had no way of knowing the depth of my envy of her and West. Even from my vantage point now, having had sixty years and more to examine myself, I still find it hard to understand my need for praise and fear of blame with West and Olivette Normandin in those days at the end of the war. I suppose we develop our final personality over time, not all at once, and people and places and events make their marks on us—or our genetic makeup deals with these elements in a certain way, the old nature-nurture riddle. I had dealt with other "authority figures" back at home and later in the army; some had made me feel stupid or ignorant, but none of them had made me feel small and insignificant. I didn't really care that I couldn't be a decent carpenter or mathematician or engineer, but I did care, very much, about being like West and Olivette Normandin, even though I couldn't quite say what that meant.

"I have a few books I always carry with me," she said, "just reference books, but they have illustrations. You may borrow them if you like."

I said, "Thanks, I'd like that."

"Unfortunately, they're in French. Is that a great problem?"

"I think I can get by," I said, knowing that I was probably fooling myself and not sure that I was fooling her. My sense of inadequacy wasn't helped by knowing that her English grammar was better than mine. Even in later years I had never quite lost the awe I felt then for people who moved easily back and forth between languages. I could never quite decide whether Conrad was simply a great novelist or a great novelist because he was writing in a second language.

"Perhaps you will be killing two birds with one stone, as you Americans put it, learning something about art and refreshing your knowledge of French." And then she smiled and added something in French which, only years later, I finally understood: *Faire d'une pierre deux coups*: kill two birds with one stone. Though I didn't know what she'd said I knew she was joking about something, and I was pleased to be a part of it.

West and two other officers—one a lieutenant, the other a captain—came down the entrance stair and stopped for a minute at the foot. The captain had a clipboard with papers on it, and he was pointing something out to West and the lieutenant. After a moment West shook hands with them and came over to us. We were still sitting on the truck bumper with our canteen cups.

"I see you've been living it up," he said. "Having a pre-dinner drink?"

"Yes, and hoping for dinner," Olivette said.

"Warm C-rations," West said, "which you'll have to admit are better than cold K-rations. Plus the wine of the locale, of course." We would go back to Fussen, he explained, and eat there with an armored unit and bunk there for the night. "There's work to be done here," he went on, "packing and crating and sorting. But we can't move anything till we have more trucks and some place to move the things to. Probably Munich, but not for a while. We're going on tomorrow to a place called Altaussee and have a look. They tell me we've never seen anything like it."

West was right about the warm C-rations, though if there was local wine I didn't see it. A Military Government (MG) unit had already moved into Fussen and taken over some houses and the few municipal buildings like the post office and city hall. I didn't see where the MG people put up West and Olivette for the night. I bunked in with other drivers in a barn that belonged to a farm on the outskirts of the village. The hay still smelled like cows, and there were cow patties in the pasture by the barn where we parked our vehicles, but there was a well with a pump and some big tins that we used for baths. It was May, but the nights were still cold, and we snuggled into the hay and worried about the smell later.

In the morning, after more warm C-rations, I brought the truck into the main street by the post office and waited for West and Olivette. It was a beautiful, bright morning, with a light haze on the mountains already beginning to burn off. I knew we would be heading south and east, into those mountains. I hadn't yet come to terms with the place I was in. I still couldn't quite believe that the castle and the lake and the mountainside weren't make-believe, some preposterous setting for some preposterous movie. But if all this was real, I thought, then who could tell what might come next? If Cinderella's castle was real, why not Hansel and Gretel's cottage or Jack's beanstalk? As it turned out, there *was* a fairyland quality about Altaussee: an underground city that might have been dug by Tolkien's dwarves. But the factual reality of what was in that city was more fantastic than the city itself.

We left Fussen and immediately began to climb in long grades that were so gradual we hardly knew we were going up. But by the time we got to the village of Altaussee, West estimated that we must be at a height of about seven-thousand feet. We kept on through the village, and after a mile or so we stopped climbing and came out onto a wide, flat shelf of land that looked as if it had been cut out of the mountain. We saw buildings there, large, square three-story buildings that looked as if they had been transplanted from the factory section of an industrial city. There were Third Army jeeps and half-tracks parked near the buildings and GIs with their M-1s slung standing guard at doorways.

"I'll go see what the drill is here," West said. He got out of the truck and Olivette and I watched as he went up to the main doorway. The GI on guard there saluted him, and West returned the salute and went inside.

"He doesn't salute like an officer," I said to Olivette. The officers I knew expected crisp, formal salutes from enlisted men, but their return salutes were casual, hardly more than a little wave of the hand. West had saluted more like an enlisted man.

"He's not comfortable being an officer," Olivette said. "In fact, he's not comfortable being a soldier at all."

I didn't know what to make of that. "Well, most of us are civilian soldiers," I said. "Is that what you mean?"

We watched as the GI at the doorway snapped to attention for a full colonel and got a hand wave salute in return.

"After a while you civilian soldiers accept being soldiers," she said. "He doesn't accept that. He plays the game of being a soldier, but he knows it's only a game. He never forgets that. He is always only himself."

Because I took all general comments personally, I felt as if she had said: You're like all the others; you enjoy being a soldier; it gives you a kind of identity; you're not like West. It's terrible to be nineteen and unsure of yourself. I wasn't sure I even knew what she meant by the remark, but I knew she meant it as a compliment to West, a way of saying he was someone special, and I knew in my heart that it must be just one more way that I wasn't like West.

West came back to the truck and leaned into the cab and looked up at us. "I've talked to our Monuments people in there," he said. "This is the big casino, the mother lode. None of us will ever see anything like this again." He held out his hand to Olivette and helped her out of the truck. Then he said, "Come on, Jimmy," and my heart jumped, because I had been sure I was going to be left behind again.

I jumped down next to them, and West put one arm around Olivette's shoulders and the other around mine and pulled us together in a little huddle. "They're being tough about who gets in," he said, "but I know the main man. He'll wink if we play the game right." He looked at me with apparent seriousness. "There are DPs in there: Hungarian, Polish, Russian, you name it. How's your Polish, Jimmy?"

I said we lived near Hamtramck and I knew the Polish words for "hello" and "how are you" and the name of the Ash Wednesday doughnuts.

"Good enough," he said, "you're our Polish interpreter."

The GI guard saluted West again as we went through the main doorway, but this time I didn't look at West's return salute. We crossed a wide room with a few chairs and desks and went through a doorway on the far side. We were inside the mountain by then; the air was cooler, as if we had walked into an air conditioned room. Two Third Army colonels stood talking to a tall man in army fatigues with what looked like a naval insignia on his cap. When he saw West he came over and shook his hand, and West introduced him to Olivette and me. I almost didn't catch his name—Carson—because my mind was on my identity as a Polish interpreter. He pointed to a pair of narrow gauge rails set in the cement floor and running through an archway into the mine. He said they were for tram cars that ran down the main tunnel of the mine. In a minute there was a screeching noise and the sound of an engine and four miniature box cars were pushed into the room by a little gasoline locomotive. The cars were like the ones you see at an amusement park, the ones that go through the tunnel of love or the house of horrors. They were about five-feet long and maybe three feet-wide with wooden sides and no seats. A one star general and a colonel (both Third Army) crawled out of one car, and a Third Army major and a civilian out of another.

The general came over to West and Carson. "Sweet bloody Jesus," he said, "I didn't believe you when you told me about the stuff in there, and now no one'll believe me either. What in hell are you going to do with it?"

"Wrap it," Carson said, "and pack it piece by piece and take it to Munich. Sooner or later return it to where it came from."

"Take it to Munich?" the general said. "In trucks? Over those mountains?"

"That's how it got here," Carson said.

"I know Hannibal got elephants over the Alps," the general said, "but that was easy compared to this."

When the Third Army people had gone, Carson went over to a footlocker against the wall and brought out three large GI flashlights. "We have some lights down there," he said, "but they're pretty erratic." He and West got into the first car behind the engine, and I helped Olivette into the next car and got in next to her. We were sitting on bare boards. "We call them box seats," Carson said. Then, "Keep your heads low and your hands inside. Some of the overhead is low and some of the walls pretty close." He leaned over and did something with the engine and we began to move.

We hadn't got thirty yards from the room before the light began to fade. West held one of the flashlights straight ahead, like a headlight, so that we could see the track ahead. But I could also see that the roof ahead seemed to be getting lower and the walls closer to the track. I could smell the roof and the walls, an old basement odor. I could feel Olivette next to me squeezing herself lower in the box, and I knew she felt what I did, that the roof was coming down on us like the lid on a coffin and that the walls closing in on us. She said something in a low voice—I thought she said "Oh." But then she said it again—not Oh—Poe.

"The walls are moving in," she said, "but where is the pendulum?"

Then Carson spoke, his voice dead and flat and disembodied. "This is your tour guide speaking. We're in the main tunnel here. There are dozens of side tunnels leading off from this. Each one leads to a room cut out of the rock. Some of these rooms are enormous, the size of football fields and fifty or sixty feet high. Every one of them is stuffed with artworks, most of it looted, but some of it German. Paintings by the thousands, sculptures, books, jewels, rugs, tapestries. Most of it meant for Hitler's museum or Goering's mansion. These rooms even have names. There's the Kaiser Josef room, where Michelangelo's sculpture of the Madonna and Child is. And the Mineral Kabinett room, where the Ghent altarpiece is. You could stock twenty museums with the things here and still have a lot left over. We'll be packing things up here for months, won't we, Alan?"

"I'll be back to help," West's voice said. "I wouldn't miss it for the world."

"I think we'll have a look at Michelangelo first," Carson said, "one of the big stars of the show."

We went on for another minute or so, then stopped. In the light from the flashlights I could see an enormous metal door set in the rock. A placard on the door said "Kaiser Josef." Carson unlocked the door and we went in. It was hard to see how large the room was, but there were wooden racks as far as I could see, some as high as twenty feet, all crammed with paintings leaning against each other, and furniture and miscellaneous shapes in the shadows. In the middle of the floor was the Madonna sculpture, nearly life size. There were GI blankets and bedspreads and comforters on the floor next to it to be used as packing. We held our flashlights on it for several minutes. No one said anything. I wouldn't have known what to say if anyone had asked me what I thought. I don't know that I was thinking anything at all. I was just trying to comprehend that the thing was marble, because that seemed impossible to me. The features of the Virgin's face, the folds of her gown, the child's hair: I couldn't imagine that they had been cut from stone. I kept going back to the Virgin's face—the downcast eyes, the expression of her face as she looked down at her child. I had been seeing pictures of the Virgin and of Jesus all my life, most of them very bad, as I knew even then—maudlin pictures of Mary with a bleeding heart, Jesus as a kind of boy who reminded me of Shirley Temple in old movies. But this was different. I thought that if I looked at it for a long time I might be able to get past the amazement I felt at the skill of the sculptor and say why I thought it was different from the goody-goody pictures I remembered. But Carson turned off his flashlight and said it was time to move on.

Carson led us back to the tram cars, and again we moved through blackness for several minutes. Then again there was an iron door set in the rock and another room, and more wooden racks with paintings and sculptures. If you didn't know that the place held things worth millions you would have thought you were seeing someone's attic where odds and ends were stacked: old family pictures, grandpa's old favorite chair, sets of silverware long out of fashion. After a while the sheer quantity of things blurred what sense I had of their value, and I remembered what Olivette had said about Neuschwanstein—art in bulk was deadening. Of the next several rooms we saw I could later remember only two or three items specifically: one of Rembrandt's self portraits and Vermeer's painting of the artist in his studio. I could say honestly that I had seen Titians and Raphaels and Correggios, because I remembered the names, but in my memory I had only a picture like a film run too fast of saints and angels and the virgin standing, sitting, kneeling, and the Christ child lying in the virgin's lap, or sitting on her knee, or in the straw of the stable being adored by the Magi.

But the last room Carson took us to was different, the Mineral Kabinett room, where the Ghent altarpiece was. The Third Army people had strung some lights in there powered by a generator set off against one wall, but the bulbs were low wattage and they dimmed every minute or so when the generator ran rough. I had heard West and Olivette talk of the Ghent altarpiece once or twice, but I had no real idea of what an altarpiece really is. I found I was looking at several sections of wood paneling made like a privacy screen you set up between rooms. The sections folded together, and some were painted on both sides so that, even closed, there would be a picture. The parts were all separated now, ready to be packed and sent off. The panel I was looking at, the largest, was the one called *The Adoration of the Lamb,* and next to it were two small panels, Adam and Eve being expelled from Eden. Years later I saw many reproductions of the altarpiece, professional photographs with enhanced coloring, but the altarpiece that remains in my memory is the one I saw in the flickering light of the Mineral Kabinett room with West and Olivette and Carson, where the panels seemed to extend into the shadows of the racks of looted paintings.

We stood and looked in silence. The others were familiar with the piece, but it was new for me, and it was a few minutes before I could even put together what I was seeing. On a broad expanse of green, with towers and spires far in the background, crowds of people, some obviously royal, others obviously ecclesiastical, were converging from four different directions. All were dressed in robes and sandals. In the center, the point of convergence was an altar. A lamb stood on it, and around it angels knelt. The lamb seemed to have a crown that gave off light. Above, in the background, was a circle of light with a dove in its center, and light radiated from the circle down on the whole expanse of the painting. I stared at the lamb for I don't know how long before words came to me: *Agnus dei qui tollis peccata mundi,* the words from the Latin mass I had grown up with, words that had clearly meant very little to me until now. Now my mind raced: lamb of God, sacrificial lamb, washed in the blood of the lamb. I probably had seen a thousand pictures of Christ and Jesus in my nineteen years, but I couldn't remember ever seeing a picture of a lamb. I kept staring at the painting. The perspective was not right. The crowds in the rear should have been made smaller. The altar should have been foreshortened. It was a picture that a child might have painted if the child could paint what his imagination saw. The scene was a happy scene; there was joy on all the people's faces. The light beaming down from above might have been the sunlight in a child's painting. The whole thing had an air of rightness, of pleasantness, like the child's picture of his house and his family and the sun shining down on them. And then I noticed that there was a chalice on the altar in front of the lamb and that there was blood streaming from the lamb's breast into the chalice. The mass again, of course, the act of transubstantiation, wine into blood, the real presence. My theology was being dramatized before me. The only mass I'd been to in Europe had been in France, the altar the dropped tailgate of a truck. We'd all been given general absolution in case we died. While I was thinking of that, my eyes moved to the end panels of the altarpiece: Adam and Eve being expelled from Eden. None of the bright greens and reds of the other panel were here, only grays and blacks. The figures were gaunt and unhealthy looking; if there was any expression on their faces it seemed to be shock. They looked stunned as well as sick. Eve's stomach was slightly swollen, as if she might be in early pregnancy. Both had one hand covering their crotches, but I'd never seen two people who looked less sexual. If I had ever wondered what Adam and Eve looked like, I suppose I would have made them Neanderthals, but in fact I had never wondered at all, because I knew the expulsion from Eden as just a story, the subject of a thousand jokes. But it wasn't just a story for the painter of the altarpiece. They were real people who had survived a catastrophe; they had the drained look of survivors of some terrible accident.

Once again Carson's voice ended the visit. "Next time you all have to pay," he said, "no more free tours." We went back to the tram cars for the last time, and twenty minutes later we were back at the head of the line, blinking in the light, still not talking.

Olivette and I went outside while West said his goodbyes to Carson. When West came out we walked back toward the truck, West between Olivette and me, one arm around Olivette's shoulders, the other around mine. No one had spoken yet. It seemed to me exactly right that we three should be walking close together like that, because I was full of a feeling I couldn't describe except to say I had been initiated; I had survived a test, in their presence and with their help. I had presented myself before great artworks, like some African boy facing a lion, and I had, without conscious will, been touched and transported out of time and place. I had killed the lion. I had earned a minor place in their society.

Chapter 4

We bunked in for the night back in the little village of Altaussee, courtesy of Third Army. I ate C-rations with the motor pool people that night, and after dinner while I was fooling around with my truck, West came by and said he and Olivette were going to break out a couple of bottles of wine in the little room they had in the back of a pub. "We're going to drink to art," he said. "Come on by if you haven't got anything better to do."

"I will," I said, trying not to show my elation. Even better than the invitation was the casual tone of it, as if we were pals. The thought crowned my day.

I got some hot water from the cook tent, shaved and washed in honor of the event, and went looking for them. The room they'd found was a kind of storeroom behind the main room of the tavern. There were a few empty beer kegs stacked against one wall. There were wooden pallets laid on the dirt floor, and in a corner, on a pallet slightly raised, were the blankets and shelter halves we all carried for bedding.

"Not the Ritz," West said, "but—"

"C'est la guerre," Olivette finished.

"Give me a hand with the furnishings?" West said to me.

He and I shoved some empty beer kegs over to the center of the room, three for seats and one in the middle for a table. Olivette produced a bottle of wine from under the blankets and put it on the table. "No glasses," she said. "I suppose that means we must use our canteen cups again?"

I wanted to be of some use. "I'll look in the bar," I said. I went back into the bar, using my flashlight, but the Third Army GIs had already been there and the place was pretty well gutted.

The mirror behind the bar was smashed, and the handles on the beer pulls had been torn off. It seemed stupid but not really surprising. I'd seen a man rifle butt a piano in Saarbrucken. I went back to the storeroom. "No luck," I said.

"Why then, we make do," Olivette said. "We have two choices. We can fill our canteen cups and get drunk quickly, or we can drink small measures slowly, like civilized people."

West put the three canteen cups on the table keg and poured slowly and carefully into each, "In a civilized way," he said.

"Now," Olivette said, raising her cup, "let us drink to Karl Sieber."

"To Karl Sieber," West said, and raised his cup.

"To Karl Sieber," I said, though I didn't know who he was.

We drank, and then Olivette said to West, "Tell Jimmy what you told me, why we drink to Karl Sieber."

West put his cup down on the keg. "Carson told me about him," he said. "He worked in the mine restoring any damaged paintings that came in. He'd been there for years. He'd joined the Nazi party because people said he should, but he'd never had anything to do with their politics. The Austrian underground people found out the Germans were going to blow up the mine at the last moment. Hitler's orders. No artworks to survive for the Allies. The Austrians managed to find the bombs the Germans had set and got rid of them. Sieber went into the mine with small dynamite charges and blew the doors to the rooms closed so the Germans couldn't get in them."

"A true hero if there ever was one," Olivette said. "A lover of art. One thinks better of Germans because of him."

"Like Rose Valland," I said.

"Yes," she said after a moment, "I think that is a just comparison."

After that we talked about some of the things we'd seen that day, or rather they talked about them. I couldn't think of anything to contribute, but I didn't mind, didn't feel out of it. I at least knew which things they were mentioning, and I was there. That was enough.

"The Germans were at least careful with the things they stole," West said. "Something like the Ghent piece is fragile, shouldn't ever be moved at all, but they managed to move it at least twice without hurting it."

"It is a remarkable piece," Olivette said, "maybe even more remarkable for a Catholic, I suppose. You think so, Jimmy?"

"Yes," I said, "remarkable." The wine was making certain words hard to say, and I suppose it was the wine that made me say what I went on to say. I was a Catholic, I told them, but the picture hadn't reminded me of that, or at least not at first. It was the crowds of people who'd caught my attention, coming in from the four directions, people in robes and sandals, so that I knew the scene was from far in the past, but I forgot I was looking at a picture, they all seemed so interesting. It was the lamb that shocked me; it seemed so out of place, so outlandish, until I began to remember the Lamb of God, the blood of the lamb, and all that. That seemed to change the picture for me. I still liked it, but not in the same way.

"The religious part seemed intrusive, you mean?" Olivette asked. "I can understand that, I think."

"Maybe that's it," I said, "but I looked at the Michelangelo statue of the Madonna and Child and that didn't bother me."

West said, "Maybe it has to do with symbols, Jimmy. Van Eyck painted for people who weren't far away from slaughtering animals for sacrifice, so the lamb seemed a natural symbol of salvation for them. You're further along the line from them. To you the lamb seems out of place because you've lost the notion of a literal sacrificial lamb. You may see it as simply a symbol. Most people nowadays probably feel like that."

"But I still believe the same things they did," I said, "I mean about Christ as the savior and all that."

"Are you sure?" Olivette asked me. "Then maybe you should make up your own symbol, like modern artists."

"I don't want to make things up," I said, "I could never make up anything that would make Michelangelo and van Eyck use it in a painting."

"Well said, Jimmy," West said. "If the story was good enough for them it should be good enough for us. That's a very sane point of view."

"A pragmatic point of view," Olivette said. "I remember lines from your American poet, Emily Dickinson. 'Better an *ignis fatuus*/Than no illume at all—' Better a false light than no light at all. I believe she was being ironic."

"Maybe," West said, "you never know with Emily. She may have meant that all lights are false, in the sense that they're always partial. You know, Freud on the mind, or Einstein on time and space. Partial light. Always leaving a lot unexplained."

Olivette laughed. "I think that's more you than Emily Dickinson."

"Doesn't matter who," West said, "if it's true."

I went to sleep that night replaying the conversation in my mind. I'd had enough wine to make me repeat it over and over like the words of a song. I had said I believed the same things that the old artists believed, but now I wasn't sure. I had heard *"Agnus dei qui tollis peccata mundi*" a thousand times, but never once in those thousand times did I think of salvation through the lamb. The words had apparently had no meaning for me; I must have repeated them simply from habit. And West had called the whole thing a "story." For me the word *story* meant fiction, something made up, like the Adam and Eve story. But the gospel story wasn't fiction. On Good Friday at our parish school we marched around the Stations of the Cross—the betrayal in the garden, the scourging, the crucifixion—all things that were history, not fiction. And West's saying that everything we know is a false light, only a partial light. Before I dropped off I was repeating "fiction" and "crucifixion" and mixing them up: "fixion" and "crucifiction," and already beginning to feel the next day's headache from the wine.

The next morning West said, "One more stop before we go back. Berchtesgaden. I'm told that most of the loot there has already gone on to the mine here, but we'll have a look. The view will still be there at least. They couldn't haul that away."

So we piled into the truck again and headed east, still at about seven-thousand feet. I was anxious to see Hitler's place, but I knew in advance that it wouldn't mean as much to me as Altaussee. Years later when I read Tolkien's account of the mines of Moria where treasures lay buried, guarded by the race of dwarves, I wondered if Tolkien had somehow heard of the saga of Karl Sieber and the mine at Altaussee. But long before I'd read Tolkien, the mine at Altaussee had become a part of my dreams. I would feel damp and coolness again, feel myself hurtling after a single shaft of light, see again the great steel doors cut into the rock, and wonder what treasures I would find behind them. Once in a while in those later years I would take down an art book in the library and page through it until I found pictures of the Ghent altarpiece and the Michelangelo Madonna and Child, but they were always disappointing. I missed the shadows that the poor lighting at Altaussee had thrown on the Madonna's face, and the book made the reds and greens of the altarpiece too vivid. It didn't matter to me that the pictures I was seeing were more accurate than the real things I had seen years before. What I saw in the salt mine would always be the norm for me. And I was middle-aged before it occurred to me that I had spent half my life comparing people I knew to West and Olivette Normandin and had always found those people lacking.

The road was narrow and winding but well banked, and though I was sure we were climbing, the grades were so gradual that often I couldn't be sure whether we were going up or down. I kept looking off from the road at the mountains, thinking about the last redoubt. Apparently it hadn't existed except in rumor and in our frightened imagination, but as you looked at the incredible heights and the bottomless ravines it was easy to see how the myth had begun. Armor would be useless. An attacking army would have to come on foot, mile by mile, maybe even yard by yard. Once you got close enough to shoot, your own artillery and bombing would be useless. It would be an infantry war, the worst kind.

The town of Berchtesgaden was like the other alpine towns we had seen, nestled in green at the foot of mountains, so picturesque that it looked like a postcard. American paratroopers were in charge when we got there, the 101st Airborne. They had set up a roadblock at the road that led away from town and up to the Eagle's Nest. A paratrooper captain from Nebraska looked over West's credentials.

"You can go up and look around if you like," he said, "but you won't find any artwork up there. You won't find much of anything. We're blocking the road to keep our people from getting drunk and going up there and falling off."

"Have you been up there?" Olivette asked him.

"Yes, ma'am," he said. "Great view."

"There should have been some paintings there," West said, "and statuary. Maybe archives too."

"Well, the Frenchies got here first," the captain said. "They must have gone through the place like locusts through a corn field. What they couldn't take away they trashed."

We were still sitting in the truck. I didn't turn to look at Olivette, but I could sense her stiffen beside me.

"I suppose I can understand it," the captain said. "Five years they waited to get their hands on German things. But you hate to see stuff just ruined. Furniture busted up, drapes all torn down, picture frames laying around everywhere, all broken up. You said there was statuary? Lots of pieces everywhere."

"Well, we'll go up and have a look," West said.

"Some of your fine arts people are up there," the captain said, "but I don't know what there is to see." He waved to the troopers at the roadblock, and I put the truck in gear and started up the sloping road. Out of the corner of my eye I saw West's hand on Olivette's knee, patting it. I wished I could have said or done something like that, could have said, I know how you feel, someone in my company smashed a piano. But I didn't say it. I suppose I thought it would presume too much.

In a minute or two my mind was taken over by the road. It seemed to me barely wide enough for the truck, so steep I had to go to low gear and front wheel drive, and even then we were barely moving. I could feel myself leaning left, into the mountain, and I thought I could feel Olivette leaning toward me. You had to lean that way; it was like gravity. If you looked to the right you could see only space, seemingly under the truck, and once in a while on a curve a glimpse of the road you'd just come over, a tiny curl of pavement over sheer nothing. I kept saying to myself, "The Germans hauled supplies up this road; it's not as bad as you think." But I didn't believe that. I clutched the steering wheel in a near death grip and forced myself not to turn left into the mountain. A voice that didn't sound like Olivette's usual voice was saying something over and over in French. Finally our road curved one last time, to the left, to a break in the mountain wall and onto ground that was blessedly flat and even more blessedly wide. I stopped the truck and we sat for several minutes. I took my hands off the wheel and tried to get the cramps out of my fingers.

Finally West broke the silence with a joke. "I heard you praying," he said to Olivette. "The Americans say there aren't any atheists in foxholes. Maybe we can add a variation of that now."

Olivette laughed, but when she spoke her voice shook a little. "We atheists have a limited vocabulary," she said. "When we swear we have to use God's name. And when we're afraid, we use the words we learned as children." She turned to me and put a hand on my arm. "You didn't say anything," she said, "you just kept driving. Weren't you afraid?"

"I was paralyzed," I said. "I wanted to get out and hug the wall and creep the rest of the way."

"You didn't, though," she said.

I said, "I told myself other people had done it. I suppose I was ashamed not to do it too."

"Jimmy's an honest young man, Olivette," West said. "You should know that by now."

I could feel the muscles in my arms and shoulders beginning to relax, but I knew too that the feeling of ease and warmth came partly from having been noticed and touched and joked about. It was pleasant to feel that we three had shared danger together, almost like comrades.

A jeep was parked forty yards across from us where the mountain rose up again and led to the Eagle's Nest. I drove over and put the truck next to the jeep. A paratrooper corporal got out of the jeep and came over and saluted West. "How'd you like the white knuckle ride up?" he asked.

"Not our favorite route," I said.

"I drive it twice a day," he said, "but it never gets any better. You carrying a load?"

"No, we're empty."

"That's good. Going down's a bitch on the brakes, even in low gear. That's the bad news. Good news is there's an elevator from here on up. I'll show you."

What he showed us was hard to believe. I had been amazed at what had been done in tunnels in Altaussee, but the elevator to Hitler's Eagle's Nest seemed in a class of its own. Its shaft was cut through solid rock, of course, but the elevator wasn't the usual small working elevator you find in mines; it was like a living room, with room for dozens, with walls and ceiling that looked like gold, though they were probably copper or bronze plated. There had been some graffiti on the walls, the sergeant told us, but it had been cleaned up. I had been amazed at the richness of ornamentation I had seen at some of the English cathedrals, had even thought maybe that some of it was overdone—too much stained glass, an excess of marble in statuary and baptismal fonts, for example. But those things had at least had the intention of honoring something—God or a saint or a sacrament. But Hitler's elevator seemed sheer pointless opulence, honoring nothing but power and money. "Rose Valland told me that Hitler had no taste in art," Olivette said. "He collected what other people said was valuable. I wonder if this elevator was his idea."

We stepped out of the elevator into a large room that seemed even larger because it was almost bare. A massive conference table lay on its side, one leg broken off. A red sofa bled stuffing from several gashes. Three or four empty picture frames leaned against overturned desk chairs. But your eyes went immediately to the windows. The room was roughly square; there were tall windows on three sides, and even from a distance you could look through the windows at the mountains.

"It's like being in a lighthouse on top of the world," Olivette said.

Without thinking, we went toward the nearest windowed wall, like some kind of insects drawn to the light. French doors opened out onto a balcony; we stepped out onto it and were standing where, in a thousand pictures, Hitler had stood with Goering and Mussolini and Rommel and had planned the thousand-year Reich. We went to the balcony railing and looked. We had been seeing mountains for several days now, but this was different. Now we were above the mountains, not looking up in awe but looking down with some odd sense of superiority and mastery.

"When the devil wanted to tempt Christ, he took him to the top of the mountain," West said. "It's not hard to see why, is it?" No, it wasn't. I listened to West and felt he was saying what I only felt. He said, "Imagine Hitler standing here, feeling what we're feeling, this sense of aboveness, this exaltation. We three are extras in this great drama of the war, not protagonists. We have no power; there's nothing in us to utilize this exaltation, this hint of power. We can't be tempted, not because we're too powerful but because we're too weak. But Hitler came here to this spot on the balcony through power, not luck or chance. He could be tempted simply because he was powerful."

"And he fell," Olivette said. "Don't forget that. Don't make excuses for him."

"I don't make excuses for him," West said mildly. "None of us three would have done what he did. On the other hand, it's very possible that Hitler may have resisted temptations that we can't resist."

Olivette turned to me. "Jimmy, you see before you a man who is simply being perverse. I believe he was trained by Jesuits."

At the time I didn't know what she meant by the reference to Jesuits, but I did understand that she thought he was simply being argumentative. I knew how she felt. I'd felt the same way a few times. But I was an observer now, not a participant, and it seemed to me now that

West wasn't being perverse or argumentative. He was just being himself, as Olivette had said. It seemed to me that his mind worked in a certain way, circling around an object instead of going straight at it, so that he saw things differently than we did. People like Olivette and me were predictable, but West was not.

West laughed. "And you, Olivette, have never got past Voltaire."

"I take that as a compliment," she said.

A paratrooper lieutenant came out onto the balcony. He had a large cardboard file folder tucked under one arm. "Are you enjoying the view, lieutenant?" he asked. He looked at me and added, "We have one lower down for the enlisted men."

"My God, you must be joking!" Olivette said, instantly angry. But then she looked at West and at me and saw that we were laughing.

"Sorry, Ma'am," the lieutenant said, "I thought you all knew the joke."

"It's from a Mauldin cartoon in *Stars and Stripes,*" I told Olivette. "Two officers are looking at a great view, and one of them says, 'Is there one for the enlisted men?'"

"Well, okay," Olivette said. "Maybe I should read *Stars and Stripes.*"

The paratrooper lieutenant took a large envelope out of the file he was carrying and handed it to West. "These are copies of some snaps some of our people took up north. There's a covering note with them. I think you'll find them interesting. They're kind of interlocking. You'll need a place to spread them out." He looked out over the parapet, then back at the room inside. "This may be a very appropriate place to look at them. You can give them back when you're done with them."

"Right," West said. "We'll look them over now."

I don't think any of us were anxious to leave the balcony to look at pictures, but we went back into the littered room. There were broken up tables here and there but nothing that would stand up by itself. Finally we went over to the interior wall and used a flat piece of plaster to sweep a spot clean. West opened the envelope and took out a typed sheet and read it; when he'd finished it he looked off toward the mountains for a moment, as if thinking, and Olivette and I tried to read his face. Then he said, "The lieutenant was right. This is a good place to see these pictures."

He knelt down about three feet from the wall and began taking the pictures out of the envelope. "They're numbered on the back," he said, "to keep them in order." He began placing them face up on the dusty floor, and Olivette and I knelt down on the floor next to him.

At first I didn't know what to make of them. They looked like pieces of a picture puzzle that had to be put together. And as West explained, that's really what they were.

"They're flash pictures from a mine up north, called Bernterode," he said. "Some of our people have been in there. They took these pictures before anything was moved, the way police do at a crime scene. They didn't have a wide angle lens, so they just moved the camera around in a circle. You see there's some duplication."

He had arranged the photos in the order they were taken, and as I realized this I began to piece together the overall picture. But even then I wasn't sure what I was seeing. It seemed to be a room of some kind, with dark, shadows everywhere from the flashes. There were four things that seemed to be coffins arranged on some platform or table. One of them had a wreath on top. Flags or banners with symbols I didn't know were hanging, apparently from a ceiling. Another banner had Hitler's name in large letters, and around it a sequence of swastikas.

"Is it Hitler's funeral?" I asked. "Why the four coffins?"

"Not Hitler's funeral," Olivette said, "something more revealing about the German mind."

"Or about the Nazi mind at least," West said. "One of our people with the First Army found the place. What you see in the pictures is a room they found in a potash mine. It's clearly a room they just made; it's walled off from a main passage with new bricks. There are lots of odd things there beside the coffins—ceremonial swords and helmets, royal crowns, lots of regal paraphernalia. Plus lots of loot, mostly pictures. The banners are German regimental banners. But the coffins take the cake." The First Army people had assumed, West said, that one of the coffins would be Hitler's, but when the experts had time to examine them they found that the first coffin held the remains of Field Marshal von Hindenburg; the second, the remains of his wife; the third, the remains of Frederick the Great; and the fourth, the remains of Frederick William the First. "It was a mausoleum of German history," West said. "The people who made it were determined that the memories of Germany's greatness would survive. Sort of a time capsule."

"But whoever opened the place up would find looted artwork, not just German funerary things," Olivette said. "I suppose whoever made the place would think of the loot as just the spoils of war."

"I suppose," West said. "It's hard to read the mind of someone who would make a collection like that."

"Really?" Olivette said. "I think the mind is quite easily read. It's a fanatic's version of the traditional German military mind. You don't see any relics of Goethe or Beethoven there, do you? It's all military—the thing most important in German history."

I didn't know who Frederick the Great or von Hindenburg were, but I could guess their importance from West's account. I watched Olivette's face, and I knew she wasn't joking this time.

"The German military mind?" West repeated. "Or the Nazi military mind? Surely there's a difference."

"The Nazis didn't start the last world war," Olivette replied. "The Nazis didn't start the Franco-Prussian War. The Nazis didn't write the bible on war. Clausewitz did."

West didn't say anything for a moment, and I wondered how he'd respond. Olivette's references meant nothing much to me, but I knew they did to her and West. I was uncomfortable, like a child present while his parents are arguing.

Finally West said, "I take your point. Only a fool disputes history." He paused for a moment. "I was thinking about Jimmy and myself—" He nodded toward me. "Thinking that we're Americans, and I'm wondering what sort of time capsule we'd build if we knew that the war was lost for America, what we'd put in it for later Americans to find. Something that would suggest how they should start over." I felt as if I hadn't read my history assignment and was about to be called on. All I could think of was the flag and "The Star Spangled Banner."

But West, thank God, went on without me. "I think Jimmy and I would agree that what we wanted to preserve would be documents—the Constitution and the Bill of Rights, and maybe the Declaration of Independence."

Olivette glanced at me, but I had nothing to say, only wore an expression that I hoped meant I agreed with West. "I suppose you'd like to know what a Frenchwoman would put in the time capsule," she said, and I was glad to see that she was smiling. "Well, we have a constitution too, you know, and I suppose I'd put that in. But I assure you I wouldn't put in bodies or banners or swords. Maybe along with the constitution a Watteau and a set of Edith Piaf records and a bottle of good French wine."

After that we sat back on the floor and were silent for a while. I knew we were all thinking the same thing. You couldn't easily measure the difference between the room in the pictures and the room we sat in now: the coffins, the banners, the sacred insignias in the one room; the torn tapestry, the broken picture frames, the dust that had been statuary and ornament in the other. Two endings: one imagined, one real.

"I suppose I sound very righteous condemning the German mind," Olivette said, "considering that my countrymen looted the place we're sitting in."

"Well, if that saddens you, Olivette," West said, "then be saddened for the history of the species. All sides loot in a war. We're all in this together, you and Napoleon, the Germans and Hitler, we Americans and Sherman and Sheridan. Americans have even savaged our own people, Olivette."

We were sitting cross legged on the floor, like three Buddhas facing each other. I said, "Maybe all sides do, but not everybody on all sides. We three haven't looted anything." I hadn't meant to say "we three," as if we were the three musketeers, but it had slipped out.

"Ah, the mystery of personal virtue," West said. "Or is it that we three haven't really been tempted? What if I had a chance to steal a Vermeer?"

"Ah, you're back explaining Hitler again," Olivette said. "I really think you're a Calvinist even though you don't go to church. I think you believe we're all fallen creatures, condemned by original sin."

West smiled. "That's a comforting thought, isn't it? We don't have to worry about being bad; we just can't help ourselves. But then why do we condemn Hitler? Do we say, we're all fallen, but he's more fallen than we are?"

"Ah, Jesuit logic chopping again," Olivette said. "Don't take him seriously, Jimmy."

But of course I did take him seriously. I was nineteen and not at all sure of my moral moorings, but I found myself arguing that everything about the scene called for meaning. I may have been, as West had said, an extra in the drama of the end of the war, but even an extra is aware of the great movements of the plot. I had stood where Hitler had stood on top of the world. I had seen in pictures the failed dream of the Reich. I had seen two countries destroyed. I had seen old people and children eating from garbage cans. I had seen men from my own company rape and loot. I had seen these things in a kind of passive, almost dream-like way, but West had made me think about them, and I was wondering now if I and my country were superior in some way besides winning a war. I was not important, but the thing I wanted to know was important. I was thinking, and I was listening.

"We should probably get going," West said, "unless we want to be up here in the dark."

"I want to look at the mountains again," Olivette said, "from outside, where Hitler saw them."

So we went back out onto the balcony. It was getting late in the afternoon. The mountain tops were still in bright sunlight, but the greens further down the slopes were beginning to darken. We leaned against the heavy concrete railing and simply stared for several minutes. West said, "Makes you think better of the nature poets, doesn't it?"

"Or the nature painters," Olivette said. "You can see why they'd want to paint this. Of course, they'd give their picture a title, wouldn't they, to give the scene a meaning."

I thought about that as we turned away to go inside. Years from now, I thought, if I'm describing this thing to someone, how will I explain what I felt here? We looked at Hitler's mountains, I'd say, and the war had just ended, and everything was shot to hell, and I wanted to say something profound to the people I was with, but I couldn't find the words now because I was already thinking of driving back down that damned cliff and I knew I wouldn't be next to the mountain but on the other side, next to the abyss.

We rode the magnificent elevator down to where we had parked. The paratrooper lieutenant was waiting for us, and West gave him the pictures. The jeep driver smiled at me and said, "We'll follow you down. That's so if you burn out your brakes you won't run us over."

"He's a comedian," the lieutenant said. "On the other hand, he's got a point."

"We're not worried," Olivette said. "We have a champion driver."

I didn't feel like a champion, though I was grateful for Olivette's cheerleading. In the elevator I had devised a strategy for the run down the cliff, and I was rehearsing it now. I would put the right front fender an inch away from the mountain wall, and I would hug the curve of the wall like a leech. I would look at nothing but the fender and the wall; the fender and the wall would be my world. I put the truck in low gear and front wheel drive and inched over to the start of the slope. In twenty minutes it was over and I could take my head out of the vise that had kept me from looking to my left. Olivette leaned out over West and waved at the jeep behind us. "You see, no problem," she shouted, "we have a champion!" I could have kissed her.

We bunked in that night with the Airborne people. They had taken over a good sized gasthaus. The individual rooms were for officers; the dining room and parlor were for the enlisted men. I took my blankets into the parlor after chow and looked for a space to bed down. There were two sofas, but they had already been spoken for by sergeants. The room was carpeted, though, and I dropped my blankets in a corner away from the entrance and got ready for sleep. I supposed West and Olivette had got one of the officers' rooms. Wherever we'd gone so far they had stayed together, but I'd never been present when they made their arrangements with the people we stayed with. I wondered what the paratroop lieutenant, or whoever did the housing chores, thought of West and Olivette. Did they think Olivette was West's girlfriend, sweetheart, wife? Or just a wartime pickup? It wasn't a question I could answer for myself. I didn't know what status to give Olivette either. Back in the beginning I hadn't wanted to think of her and West just shacking up. That was a term I understood to apply to certain women—DPs, and camp followers, and the like, but not to Olivette—but I had no term for her, and I wanted one.

Later that night I woke up and had to go to the john. It was just a closet, like a clothes closet, down a hallway. You opened the door and realized it was just an indoor outhouse, with a bucket of water on the floor and a dipper to throw water down the hole when you were through. I went padding through the hallway in my socks, trying to be quiet, but the floors were old and everything creaked. Some of the room doors were ajar because the floors were so uneven, and on the way back from the toilet I glanced into one room. There was just enough moonlight for me to see West and Olivette huddled together in an old double bed with high brass bed posts. They looked like a mattress ad. She was curled up on her right side facing the wall, and West was curled up against her, as if they were matching parts of something. I went on by in a moment. I'd always supposed they slept together, of course, but I'd never tried to visualize it. As if answering someone, in that dark hallway, I whispered, "It's all right, I know them, they're not just shacking up."

Chapter 5

The next day we went back the way we had come, to Altaussee and then back north to Neckarsulm. That meant coming down from the mountains, of course, back to the easy gradations of southern Bavaria. I believe we were all thinking the same thing: that we were leaving one sort of reality for another. Looking out eastward from the Eagle's Nest, we had been in touch for a while with Hitler's imagination, and a few minutes later we had seen the funeral photos suggesting a grandeur of failure that he probably would have approved. Out of the mountains now, back on lower ground where we felt more at home, we could look back at the experience and try to explain it to ourselves.

"We're rather like people leaving a theater after a tragic play," Olivette said, "except that I don't feel what I'm supposed to feel—what is it? Cleaned? Refreshed? Renewed? What is it in English?"

"'Purged,'" I said. "At least that's the word we used when we studied *King Lear* in school. We had to read Aristotle's work on tragedy. I never really knew what he meant when he said that we felt purged after a tragedy though."

West laughed. "I'll bet there were jokes about Ex-Lax when your teacher used the word catharsis, weren't there?"

"Ex-Lax and lots of other things," I said.

"Excuse me," Olivette said, "I don't know what this Ex-Lax is."

So West explained about Ex-Lax, and then went on to say that it wasn't a literal purging that Aristotle meant. You identified with a person like Lear; you wanted his daughters to love him; you made his mistakes and bad judgments your own, and so you suffered what he suffered. It was as if you'd done these things. You saw into yourself that way.

"Well, we didn't see a play, of course," Olivette said. "But if someone wrote a tragedy about Hitler I don't think I could identify myself with him. I can't see anything redeeming in him. I've read *Mein Kampf*; he was hateful from the start and I believe he was mad at the end."

"It would certainly take a great dramatist to pull it off," West said. "But Hitler was human. That means he was one of us. We can't disclaim him. He's not a different species." When Olivette started to say something about Jesuit logic again, West held up his hand in front of her like a traffic cop. "If you saw a play about St. Francis of Assisi you probably couldn't identify with him either. He was too good for us. We can't imagine being that good. But he's our species too."

"It's a good thing for America that you don't run the country," Olivette said. "Not even murderers would be in jail."

West laughed. "We're all part of the definition," he said, "you, Jimmy, me, Hitler, St. Francis. More likenesses than differences."

We got back into Neckarsulm late that night, and when I put the truck back in the motor pool and finally turned in it seemed to me I'd been away for a long time. I went to sleep at once and didn't think I dreamed at all, but when I woke in the morning I had the feeling that I'd just come down from a great height, and I was grateful that the floor was so level.

I didn't hear from West that day. I spent my time changing the oil in the truck and shooting the breeze with the motor pool sergeant. There'd been some news while I was away. The Military Government people had come to town, and I'd already seen several GIs and two officers wearing AMG arm bands.

"They're gonna reconstruct German civilization," the motor pool sergeant said. He was from Kentucky, near the Tennessee border, and wasn't a fan of formal education. "They're gonna run the Germans through a sieve and filter out the Nazis," he said, "and then they're gonna start from scratch and dee-mocratize the country."

He was right. Our battalion commander called together all of us he could find later that day. We formed up in a soccer field on the edge of town, and he lectured us with a bullhorn. The purpose of the AMG, he told us, was to take over the functions of the town government until we had screened out the worst of the Nazis and replaced them with the best of the Nazis. (He didn't believe there were no real anti-Nazis, except maybe infants.) This meant that we were to be policemen, judges, medics, even de facto politicians running the civil affairs of the town. And we were of necessity going to be their grocers as well. The local farms were mostly ruined or abandoned; the meat markets and grocery stores had nothing to sell. The townspeople would be on army rations, and of course that meant army overseers, another level of bureaucracy. The key positions would be held by AMG personnel, but many of us would be called on for various tasks. "Above all," he yelled into the bull-horn, "you are all to be TEACHERS. You are to teach these people DEMOCRACY in everything you do and say. You are to be MODELS for them to follow. But you will keep your relations with them to a MINIMUM. You will not have SOCIAL RELATIONSHIPS with these people. Any FRATERNIZATION will be punished." When he had finished, someone said, "Fucking isn't fraternization if you keep your hat on and don't smile."

The next day West came down to the motor pool. I was sitting in the bed of my truck, not hiding but not in plain sight of the motor pool sergeant, looking through one of the the art books Olivette had given me. He leaned against the back of the truck and looked in at me and said, "Glad to see you're improving your mind."

"Madame Normandin said I'd develop taste if I worked at it," I said, "but I think it'll be slow." It felt odd to refer to Olivette as Madame Normandin, but I didn't know what else to call her.

"Olivette is always worth listening to," he said, smiling. "She's what the French call a formidable lady." He paused, then added, "In fact, I think we might even call her a force of nature."

"I think she's great," I said. I couldn't match the easy, half joking tone he always used with her, or about her. I envied his cleverness, his way of being affectionate without show. I could only say she was great.

He sat down on the end of the truck bed and leaned against the side boards, as if he were getting settled for a long chat. "You and I are of one mind about Olivette," he said. "I agree with your adjective 'great'." He sat silent for a moment. "Once in a great while you meet someone—a woman or a man, it doesn't matter which—who's what they call 'simpatico.' That person draws you out, and you feel that you draw that person out as well." He looked at me. "You know what I mean by drawing someone out?"

"I guess so," I said. "Finding out what someone thinks."

"Yes, and finding out what you yourself think as well. Olivette stirs things up. She's an action that demands reaction. You can't be passive in Olivette's presence."

I was nineteen, and I had seen them in bed together, and so it was hard for me not to find something sexual about what West was saying. And I'd become much aware of Olivette's physical presence in the truck beside me on our trips. But something more than that in what West said rang true for me. It was what I'd meant when I said she was great. If she hadn't drawn me out, it was because there wasn't anything much in me to be drawn out, but she had given me the art book as the beginning of something worth drawing out, and she had championed me in Berchtesgaden when I had been frightened, and she had fought the Nazis for the sake of art. She was more than real for me; she was like a movie star. I didn't use the word loosely: she was great.

"But I didn't come here just to sing Olivette's praises," West said. "The military government people want Olivette and me to put together some art lessons for the children here. The children aren't in school now because we've taken away all their textbooks—vetting them for Nazi content. So until we provide some new textbooks that don't praise Hitler and the National Socialist movement the children have nothing to do. We're to show some pictures and talk a little about painting and sculpture. All without any reference to the Nazis or the war or Hitler, of course. The military government people seem to think talks about art will fill the gap until real education can begin again."

I said, "Does that mean no more trips?" After Altaussee and Berchtesgaden, Neckarsulm and German school children seemed pretty flat and uninteresting. Worse, I might be sent back to regular duty.

"I think we'll still have to get down to Heilbronn," West said, "and I've heard about some things over in Garmisch that I think we should look into. But in the meantime you're to be our technical person."

I said, "Technical person?" But I didn't care what he meant, because I knew I'd still be with him and Olivette, whatever it was.

"The AMG people found some slides in the local library when they were examining the books. And there's a projector. We thought you'd be the perfect person to run the projector," West said.

"Okay," I said. "I guess I can handle that. I might even learn something."

West laughed. "You might learn some German. My German isn't up to lecturing, and neither is Olivette's. A German school teacher is going to translate what we say."

That afternoon we went over to the school, a fairly new building in the center of town. The room we were to use had good-sized tables and movable chairs, not quite adult size. On the walls were pictures of mountains and lakes and farms and pretty country towns. They were bland and innocuous, like pictures on a calendar. I supposed that the AMG had put them up. The room looked like a classroom for children up to the age of maybe ten or eleven, and I wondered what pictures had been there before the AMG had changed them. We found the projector in a cabinet in the back of the room, and on the front wall a large map of Germany hung from a retractable coil. We retracted the map and found there was a blank screen that could be pulled down. West found some boxes of slides that he took with him so that he and Olivette could sort them out.

"Class at 9 A.M. sharp," he said.

"I'll be there," I said. "I'm looking forward to it." And I was. I was a part again of what they were doing, and I had been invited.

I got there a half hour early next morning and set up the projector and focused it on the screen. West and Olivette were putting the slides in order. A heavyset man of about sixty—our German interpreter—stood beside the screen and talked to some of the children in the first rows of seats. There were about thirty children in the room, sitting quietly, watching the three strangers. Most of them looked about ten or eleven years old; two or three might have been in their early teens.

The class began with Olivette standing by the screen and making a little speech to the children—a halting speech because every sentence had to be respoken in German by the interpreter. She said that very soon their regular classes would resume, and that in the meantime she and West—whom she referred to as Professor West—would talk to them a little about some of the great artworks from all over the world but particularly from the part of the world that they lived in—by which she meant Europe, she said, including Germany of course. The children watched her attentively as she spoke; even when the German man translated they continued to look at her, not him. Somehow they knew she was not American, I thought; it might have been her ragtag uniform, or simply her looks and the way she carried herself. West and I were clearly Americans, but she was an exotic, and since she was traveling with Americans she was most likely French. They may have been too young to have developed notions of national stereotypes, I thought, but surely they felt a difference between a person from a nation they had conquered and a person from a nation that had just conquered them.

The first slides were pictures of famous ruins—Stonehenge, Pompeii, Hadrian's Wall. The room was not dark enough for the pictures to stand out sharply on the screen, but the children seemed to be paying attention. It may have been the nearest thing to movies that they had seen in months. With Olivette and West alternating as commentators, I began projecting slides of paintings and engravings and sculptures in rough chronological order. Leonardo's *Mona Lisa* and *The Last Supper.* Bosch's *Garden of Earthly Delights*. Michelangelo's *Pieta*. Raphael's *Portrait of A Young Man*. Durer's *Four Horsemen of the Apocalypse*. Giorgione's *The Tempest.* Rembrandt's *The Night Watch.* Vermeer's *Study of a Young Woman.* Degas' *Prima Ballerina.* Like the children, I was seeing most of these works for the first time, and I could think of a thousand questions I wanted to ask West and Olivette. But the children were mostly silent during the showing. There were a few oohs and giggles at Bosch's depiction of the ugliness of human behavior, and two or three were surprised to learn that *The Last Supper* is painted on a wall and can't be moved. The only child to ask a direct question was a girl of about ten. When the showing was over she said something to the German interpreter, and he translated for us.

"The girl wishes to see the Raphael picture again," he said.

"No problem," West said, and I went back over the slides till I found it, and projected it again on the screen.

The girl looked hard at the screen for a moment and said something to the interpreter.

"She says her uncle has that picture," he said. "No doubt a copy, a reproduction."

"Probably," West said. "Well, I guess class is dismissed."

The children began to file quietly out of the room. West went over to the little girl and knelt down next to her chair so that his head was level with hers. She looked startled, but he said something to her in German that made her smile. He beckoned to the interpreter to come over. "My German isn't good for anything but laughs," he said to the man. "I want to ask her some questions about the painting. Tell her I think she's a lovely young lady and she'd be doing me a great favor to talk to me."

The German man translated, and the girl smiled again. I put the slides and projector back in the cabinets while the three-cornered conversation went on, not loud enough for either Olivette or me to understand.

Finally West stood up and said something, apparently in German, that made the little girl laugh again, and she went out of the room. The German man watched her go, then looked at West, as if waiting for something, but West only thanked him for his help, and after a minute the man left.

"I was asking the little girl more about her uncle than about the picture," West told us. "She wouldn't know whether the painting was a copy or not, but her uncle would. But her uncle isn't here—hasn't been here for a week or more. Not since the Germans left and we came, apparently. I think we need to talk to the AMG people about the uncle."

"Surely you don't think the uncle would have the original Raphael?" Olivette asked.

"No, I don't," West said. "And even if he did it would be up to AMG and the MPs to do something about it. I want permission for us to go to his place and look at whatever picture he has. If it should happen to be the real thing we have him arrested, assuming they can find him, and we put the picture somewhere safe."

I brought my truck around and we headed for AMG headquarters. On the way, West said, "We're finding out where most of the big ticket items went—to Hitler's collection or to Goering's. But there are a few things that we know were taken away by other people and that disappeared. The Raphael's one of them. A man named Hans Frank took it from Poland, apparently to Germany, but it's dropped out of sight. It could be anywhere. Including here."

"Exciting," Olivette said. "Just think, Jimmy, if we should find it our pictures might be in the newspapers."

"Or in the art newspapers," West said, "fit audience though few."

At AMG Olivette and I sat outside the major's office while West went in. In about twenty minutes they came out together and West introduced us. The major was a stocky, gray haired man of about fifty. He hardly saw my salute because he didn't take his eyes off Olivette. "Lieutenant West and his commanding officer have told me you're an expert in art, Madame, but they didn't tell me how lovely you are," he said. He reached out and took her hand and for a moment I thought he was going to kiss it, and she must have thought so too because she pulled it back abruptly. But he continued to look at her as if they were alone in the room. I turned my head so he wouldn't see anger if he happened to look at me. I didn't know how our CO had described Olivette's relationship with West to the major—girlfriend? lover? shack job?—but the major surely knew that she somehow belonged with West. I suppose he may have thought, "An attractive French woman living with an American, well, why not with me?" It was a GI point of view. It was probably what I might have thought if I outranked West, and if I hadn't known West and Olivette.

Finally he turned away from her and spoke to us as a group. "So you three make up a kind of art posse," he said. Something he saw in Olivette's face made him add quickly, "I don't mean to be dismissive, Madame. Lieutenant West tells me that this painting is of great value, but I have to tell you that my interest in art at the moment is marginal. My life right now consists of sorting out good guys from bad guys and putting the good guys in civic jobs. And putting the bad guys in jail, if possible. We think Granz, the man you're looking for is, or was, a fairly high ranking member of the party, as well as being former burgermeister of the town. In any case, he's disappeared. If we catch him and he happens to have your painting, that'll be a bonus. But we've looked for him, and so far as we can tell, he's gone to ground." He turned to West. "You can go up there and look for yourself. His house is up on the hill. There's a very old housekeeper there who knows absolutely nothing about anything, if you can believe her. If you find him call us. The MPs will take over."

West saluted, and we turned to go. The major looked approvingly again at Olivette and said, "If you find your picture let me see it. I have an eye for beauty."

Outside, Olivette said, "*Cochon*. All pigs are the same, German or American."

"That's what I've been telling you," West said, "the great democracy of the imperfect." But I could see he was annoyed. "RHIP," he said to Olivette. When she looked puzzled, he said, "Rank has its privileges."

"Like *Le droit du seigneur*?" she said.

"Something like it," he said, "the army version."

I knew what he meant. We'd learned the phrase in history class. The teacher had said it was an example of the abuse of power, and he had quoted Lord Acton: power corrupts, and absolute power corrupts absolutely.

We went back to the truck, got directions from the MPs, and headed for the house on the hill. It was just outside the north end of town, high on the hill overlooking the river. It wasn't part of a complex like so many of the houses in town. It sat alone, a square cement building that looked more like a pill box than a house. A narrow black-topped road led up to it in easy curves and grades. I parked the truck in a little gravel court in front of the house, and we went up to the front door. It had a heavy knocker in the shape of a hammer. When West had pounded several times with it the door opened part way, and a woman peered out at us. She was small and old and wrinkled. Her hair was done up in a bun in a way that reminded me of my grandmother, and she wore the wooden clogs that so many of the German women used in place of the shoes they couldn't get.

West said good day in German and asked her if Herr Granz was home. She shook her head no and started to close the door, but West put his hand on it and held it open. Very slowly, mixing his German with English, he told her that we were American soldiers and that we needed to see Herr Granz, and that if he wasn't home we wanted to look at some of his belongings. He said all this in a pleasant, conversational way, at the same time keeping pressure on the door to keep it open.

Olivette and I were standing a little behind West. I felt Olivette touch my arm, and she said, very softly, "The window, watch the upstairs window."

The housekeeper kept saying *"Nicht hier, nicht hier"* to West, and he was starting to put a little more pressure against the door. I kept my head level but let my eyes slide up toward the second story. There was nothing, then a hint of movement, maybe only the twitch of a curtain in a breeze. Then a more deliberate movement of the curtain. We were being watched.

"Lieutenant," I said, "there's someone upstairs."

West stepped back from the door and looked up, and the woman slammed the door shut. West said, "Better get your carbine from the truck, Jimmy, just in case." He wasn't wearing his side arm.

I got the carbine and came back, looking up at the window. I could see now that it was a broad single pane of glass with no sash, like a sliding door wall. There was a tiny balcony beneath it with room for maybe a single chair. There was no movement in the window now. West pushed the door open and I went in first. I'd taken the safety off the carbine, and I could feel my heart thumping with excitement. Quite suddenly I wasn't just the driver for West and Olivette. I was the man with a gun out in front, leading the mission.

We were in a large sitting room full of over-stuffed chairs and a sofa. We could see into a kitchen in the back of the house and a kind of breakfast room off to our left. Looking up, we could see that we stood in an atrium open all the way to the roof. A balcony with a banister ran almost the width of the house, then turned sharply right. There were two doors off the balcony toward the back and a third in the part that turned and led back to the front. The third would be the door to the room with the window in front. We looked quickly around the sitting room, then the kitchen and breakfast room. No one was there, and there was no Raphael either. An outside door off the breakfast room stood half open. A stairway led up to the balcony near the third door.

We went up. I was still ahead, still had the carbine at the ready. My stomach had begun to knot up. I was remembering the training we'd had in urban fighting. You'd walk into an area with your rifle at the ready, and suddenly a figure would jump at you from above or below or the side—you couldn't anticipate it—and you had to shoot it within five seconds or you were called dead. I was afraid now that the something would come at me from the side and I would see it just in time to shoot and it would be the old housekeeper. We got to the second floor and stood outside the door to the room with the window.

"This isn't Omaha Beach," West said. "We shouldn't go in shooting if we don't have to." He went over to the door and knocked loudly on it. "If you're in there, Herr Granz, listen to me. We're Americans. We want to talk to you about a painting."

We waited for what seemed a long time. There was no sound from behind the door.

"Well, I guess—" West said.

"I smell something," Olivette said.

I did too, suddenly. Smoke. Something burning.

West shoved the door open and I went in. No one jumped at me from the side, but there was a man in front of me, unexpected, and I swung the carbine and pointed it at him. In that second, two things came clear to me: I had failed my alertness test, and the man was not armed. He was sitting in a reclining chair near the window and seemed to be looking at us. Next to his chair was what looked like a big metal washtub. What we smelled was smoke coming from something burning in the tub. When we got closer to the man we could see that he wasn't looking at us; it was simply that his face was pointed toward the doorway. He had vomited, and some of the vomit was still on his chin and on his coat lapel. His face was twisted, as if he had tried to scream at the end.

West was kneeling by the washtub, trying to see through the smoke. "He's burning it," he said, "he's burning the picture!" He had pulled off his cap and was trying to smother the flames. Olivette and I knelt beside him. I couldn't keep my eyes open in the smoke for more than seconds at a time, but I saw something about the size of a large notebook crumpling and curling in the flames. Pieces of what looked liked burned newspaper floated up from the tub. He'd probably used newspaper to start the fire. I slid the big window open, and West and I picked up the tub by its handles and put it out on the little balcony. The last fragments of Raphael's *Portrait of a Young Man*—if that's what it was—drifted on a current of air toward the Neckar River.

We looked at Herr Granz but didn't touch him. That was for the MPs and the AMG. He was wearing a civilian suit, but he'd put a swastika arm band around his right sleeve.

"So he took it with him," Olivette said, "just as Hitler wanted to do. For spite."

"I suppose he took cyanide," I said. "I've heard they all carry those pills."

"They say it's quick," West said, "but it doesn't look as if it was pleasant."

"Maybe the picture wasn't the real thing," I said. "Maybe he only thought it was. Maybe it was a copy."

"That would be a good joke on him, wouldn't it?" Olivette said. "I suppose we'll find out some day."

But of course we never did.

We liberated two bottles of white wine that the MPs had somehow missed in their earlier visit. The bottles were in a clothes closet behind a stack of old magazines in the room where the dead man sat. In the same closet was a slender plywood crate with a handle. West took a slip of paper from his pocket and glanced at it and said, "Would you say that crate is about three-by-three?"

"I guess so," I said. "Why?"

"The dimensions of the Raphael are—or were—about two-and-a-half by two. This looks like its carrying case. Pretty clumsy to be carrying around. But it came all the way from Poland if what we saw was the Raphael. The painting wasn't a canvas that could be rolled up. It was painted on a wood panel."

I looked out at the balcony, where the washtub still sat, and tried to remember if what we had smelled was wood burning. But then I thought, wood that's five-hundred years old would probably burn like paper.

We went downstairs and walked through the first floor rooms looking for the housekeeper, but she wasn't there. We shut the doors and left the place for the MPs and went back down into town. West went into AMG headquarters to report what had happened. Olivette and I sat in the truck until he came back.

"He'll send the MPs up with a body bag," he said. He looked at Olivette. "He sends his regards to you."

"Cochon," she said.

That night after chow we sat around the kitchen table in West's apartment and drank Herr Granz's wine, but Herr Granz himself was there too, in all our thoughts, spoiling the party. We had all seen our share of dead Germans, but Herr Granz's death was somehow personal. He had peeked out of his window and seen the three of us on his doorstep like avenging Fates and had immediately burned his treasure and killed himself. We hadn't wanted him; we'd only wanted a painting, and we wondered if he'd known that.

"Why suicide?" Olivette said. "He wasn't a high echelon Nazi, apparently, just a small town burgermeister. What would you Americans have done with him? Put him in jail for a few months? Put him on your blacklist? Would that be so bad? Why suicide?"

"Maybe the painting," West said. "It came from higher ups, from Frank to start with. Maybe he had connections with Goering that we would have found out about. But even so, why suicide? Better question yet: Why burn the painting? It seems to me it could have been a bargaining chip. Assuming it was the real thing."

"Spite," Olivette said. "I said it before. It's the only thing that makes any sense. A last chance to hurt people you hate."

I said, "Maybe he was like Hitler. We said back at Berchtesgaden that Hitler went for broke, put all his chips on the Reich, and if that failed everything was over, the rest of the world wasn't worth saving."

"You mean maybe this man's fantasy was as mad as Hitler's?" Olivette said. "That may be, I suppose. Maybe failure was too humiliating for him."

After a while we dropped the problem of Herr Granz and turned to the problem of the painting. Olivette wondered what Granz could have done with it if he had lived. "The things that Hitler and Goering stole were going to be exhibited," she said, "after the Germans had won the war. They weren't going to be hidden. Hitler was going to build a new museum to show the world what he'd stolen. Except that no one would say they were stolen. But what would Granz do with the Raphael? The war was over, and there wasn't ever going to be a Hitler museum where he could show it. And it would be too famous for him to sell it on the open market."

"Maybe he realized that losing the war changed everything," West said, "but he still had the painting. Maybe he didn't know what to do with it, but it was too valuable to let go. Maybe, years ahead, someone would pay ransom for it, no questions asked. I think we may see a lot of that. We have some records of Hitler's loot and Goering's loot, but there must be thousands of things stolen by other people that we don't know about. When things settle down after the war there may be the world's greatest black market in artwork."

"And in fakes, too, I suppose," Olivette said. "If we've just lost the real Raphael, someone will fake it and say they discovered it in someone's attic."

"Not only fakes of real paintings," West said, "but fakes of things that never existed. They'll be called newly discovered. New Rembrandts and Titians. Maybe new Raphaels. The Germans have blown the old art world to bits."

"If someone said he'd found a new Raphael, how would they prove it was either real or fake?" I asked.

"Chemical tests of the paint," Olivette said, "X-rays, tests to establish the age of the canvas. Things like that."

"No one could tell just by looking at the new things?"

"No one could be perfectly sure," she said. "There would be arguments."

"But if the fake is so good that it takes scientific tests to prove it's false, isn't it as good as the original?" I said.

"Ah, Jimmy," West said, "you've just touched on one of the most interesting questions in art. Where does the value of the artwork lie? In the talent of the artist? The originality of the work? The authenticity? If we could imagine a perfect copy of the *Mona Lisa*, why wouldn't it be as valuable as Leonardo's original?"

"I don't know," I said. "Why wouldn't it?"

"Because the art world—the art market—puts a money value on authenticity," West said. "If artworks had no money value, a perfect copy would be as good as the original."

"You forget something," Olivette said. "There is no such thing as a perfect copy. Though there is such a thing as a copy so good that only a professional art historian could see a difference."

I drank my wine and tried to think about the real value of an artwork, but I didn't work very hard at it. Herr Granz's wine was having a pleasant effect on me, and I was really content just to listen to West and Olivette talk about art, and to watch their faces as they talked. It seemed to me I was taking in, absorbing, without any real effort, the reality of art—its complexities, its nuances, its sheer fascination. And their faces had their own kind of appeal for me. I knew in advance when Olivette was going to make a joke: her eyes widened and the corners of her mouth turned up, and her whole expression said, "Wait till you hear this!" And West's face always had the half serious, half comic look I'd come to know so well. A stranger watching them would have known at once that they were intimate. Watching them talk together about art was like watching a love scene in a movie.

"Speaking of fakes and copies and the making of pictures," West said at one point, "you should read Henry James' stories about art and artists, Jimmy, especially the one called 'The Madonna of the Future.' It's one of the saddest and truest pictures of an artist."

"I know that story," Olivette said. "The man spends his whole life preparing to paint a Madonna but never paints a thing. I agree about its sadness at least."

"One thing I wonder about," I said. West had brought me into the conversation and I felt I wasn't interrupting, but it was the wine that made me ask what I did. "You both know so much about painting, and you love it so much—did you ever try to paint yourselves? Do you feel bad that you don't paint?" As soon as the words were out they seemed rude to me.

Olivette threw up her hands in mock horror. "Ah, the ancient question," she said. "Are we acolytes because we can't be priests and priestesses? Are we drones because we can't be queens? Are we prompters and stage hands because we can't be actors?"

"I didn't mean it like that," I said, but I suppose I really did.

"I will give you two answers," she said, "one short and one not so short. The short answer is, Yes—if we had a choice between what we are doing and being great artists we would choose to be great artists. The longer answer is, We choose to do what we do because our work keeps us in contact with great art, which we value very highly. No other profession does that."

From the precision of her answer I guessed she had answered my question more times than she wanted, and I started again to make some sort of apology, but West interrupted me.

"My turn," he said. "I tried my hand at painting, and I imagine Olivette did too." She nodded yes. "You almost have to try to do it before you can estimate how hard it is to do it well. I found out I have no talent for it—zero—no amount of training would make me a painter. I was disappointed, of course. But then it occurred to me that I loved music but that I had no talent for that either. And I loved baseball, but I learned in college I was only a mediocre athlete and I wasn't going to be like Joe DiMaggio. My point is simple: we're like other people. At a certain point we realized what our capacities were, what we could do and what we couldn't. We're not failed artists; we're just non-artists who value art."

"I guess I know what you mean," I said. "I already know I won't be a ball player. I don't know about anything else though."

"You will," Olivette said, "probably when you go to the university. That's where I chose different careers almost every week before I finally chose the right one." She watched as West refilled our wine glasses. "But about trying to paint, or draw. In our art classes at school we had contests among ourselves. Not to see whose picture was best—we were all very bad—but to see which picture had the most interesting subject, but the subject had to be French. We had pictures of the Bastille and the Eiffel Tower and the Seine bridges and Notre Dame. All very bad."

West said, "I had a professor once who made up contests to see who could create a sense of the basic human condition, either in a picture or in words. I remember that someone painted a picture of Einstein's formula for energy, more or less like Picasso."

"What was your entry," Olivette asked, "picture or words?"

"Oh, picture," West said, "though I thought of great short phrases like *In principio erat verbum*, but the professor was an atheist, and I didn't think he'd appreciate that. So I daubed out a picture, water color, of a big black blob of earth, like a swamp, and out of it three trees were growing. One was law, one was religion, and one was art. I had to label them, of course, since the painting didn't indicate what they were. The law tree was scrawny and twisted. The religion tree was big and strong and bushy, with lots of side branches. The art tree was tall and slender. It was supposed to be the most beautiful, but since I couldn't paint very well, they all looked pretty much alike, like blobs."

"What did the professor think of it?" I said.

"Well, I had to explain it, of course. The black swamp was the basic, ugly human life, and the trees were the human attempts to make sense of things—through law, or religion, or art."

"The religion tree was the strongest, though," Olivette said.

"Strongest, yes," West said, "but as my professor pointed out, none of them was very tall. He assumed that was important. I didn't disagree." After a moment he laughed and said, "You know, there's a school of philosophy that would say this discussion we're having is meaningless. If you say, I wish I had Leonardo's drawing skill, this philosophy would say Leonardo's drawing skill is part of the substantial union of Leonardo's body and soul; the drawing skill isn't a separate and detachable thing. So in order to have his drawing skill you'd have to have all the rest of the union as well. You'd have to have his genetic composition, his imagination, his sexual proclivities, his liver, his appendix—you get the idea. You'd have to have Leonardo in his homogenized, complete form. In short, you'd have to be an exact duplicate of Leonardo. But no one can be an exact duplicate of another person, probably not even an identical twin, so really what your wish amounts to is that if you wish to have

Leonardo's drawing skill, you must be Leonardo. But that is not possible."

"Not only impossible but inconvenient," Olivette said, "since Leonardo's dead."

I knew they were making a joke of my question, but I didn't care. We were having a good time together with Herr Granz's wine; that was all that counted. They both had made fun of their own early paintings, and it occurred to me for perhaps the first time that it was possible to make jokes about something important like one's own failures and deficiencies without being either maudlin or self-pitying. It would be a sign that you had grown up.

It must have been about the middle of September that we had a visit from an MP major. The war had been over for three months by then. We were still making trips to Altaussee and Heilbronn and other places to help with the packing and shipping of artworks, and once in a while we found a new looting site. My battalion had shipped out for the States in July, and I had supposed I would go with them. I had hoped for delays in shipping out, because I wanted to go home, and at the same time I wanted to stay with West and Olivette. If I was ordered to go, I would have to go, of course, but it wouldn't be my decision. So I had hoped for time, hoped that the usual foul-ups would happen and that I'd be allowed to just go on for some indeterminate time doing what I had been doing with West and Olivette.

But my company CO changed that. He'd called me in the day after the word had come out and put the decision strictly on me. I'd been on loan for so long, he said, that I'd been dropped from their rations list. He'd put me back on if I wanted him to, he said, or I could stay on loan with West. "I imagine you'll want to go home," he said, "unless you're having a hell of a lot of fun with whatever you're doing."

I said, "When do I have to decide?"

Of course he said what he thought John Wayne would have said. "Take your time, soldier. Tomorrow will do."

So I went over to the motor pool and climbed into my truck and sat there for a while and tried to sort out my feelings. The pull to go home was very strong, and now that we had atom-bombed Japan I wouldn't be in any danger of being shipped to the Pacific. Going home would in effect be the end of my army life—maybe not in a month, but soon.

Family, old friends home from their tours of duty swapping war stories, parties, gossip, girls to be met, movies: the start of a new civilian life. But the pull to stay was also strong. I stared through the windshield at nothing and worked out an equation. On one side: I wanted to go home, but I also wanted to stay. On the other side: people at home wanted me there, and the people here also wanted me here—or did they? That was the unknown in the equation. Altaussee, Berchtesgaden, Herr Granz's house: I went back over the memories that clustered around those names like a man running a film in reverse, and I knew that those shared experiences had had meaning for West and Olivette as well as for me. But everything in me said that my feelings for them were stronger than their feelings for me, that the two of them were in some way vital for me but that I was something less than that for them. No matter how I turned the thing around, I couldn't help thinking that the relationship was heavily one-sided. I let myself imagine for a moment a scene in which I walked into the kitchen where they sat at the table; I said, "My outfit is going home, and I can go with them if I want to." They looked at me in surprise, then both said—but what would they say? "Don't go, Jimmy, we need you here. It wouldn't be the same without you, Jimmy." No, even in my imagination those words were mawkish and unreal. I was disgusted with myself.

I started up the truck, checked out of the motor pool, and drove to West's apartment. I tapped on the front door, and West called to come in. They were sitting at the kitchen table, just as they had been in my fantasy, and I went into the kitchen and stood in front of them. West motioned me to a chair and said, "Coffee or wine, Jimmy?"

But I didn't move. I said, "The battalion's going home. I can go with them, but I don't have to. I can stay here." I tried to say the words matter of factly, but my voice sounded choked and unsteady to me.

Neither of them said anything for a moment. Then West said, very quietly, "What are you going to do, Jimmy?"

I said, "I don't know."

Olivette got up and came around the table and stood in front of me. She put her hands on my shoulders and looked into my face for what seemed a long time. I could feel tears behind my eyes. Then she said, "I can understand why you would want to go home, but—" She stopped.

I said, "But?"

"But we would miss you terribly," she said. "Before long we will all be going home, and we will all miss each other then. All this will be over then."

West said, "Are we voting? I vote with Olivette. How do you vote, Jimmy?"

I cleared my throat and said, "I guess I'll vote to stay then." I could feel Olivette's hands squeeze my shoulders, and then she reached up and kissed me. I left them then, because all the vital things had been said. We had voted to continue the present, though all of us knew that the present couldn't go on much longer.

It was a day or two later that the MP major came to visit. We were sitting at the kitchen table planning a trip to the Munich collecting point, with stops here and there to investigate reports of paintings that had just turned up. He wasn't an ordinary MP officer. He announced immediately that he was CID, Criminal Investigation Division, and that he reported to the Theater Provost Marshal. He was a heavyset, swarthy man named Delgado who in civilian life had been a police chief in Chicago. He looked like a man who didn't smile much, but when West introduced him to Olivette as someone who had helped Rose Valland, his face lighted up in a smile of real delight. He took her hand and held it while he said, "I'm honored to meet someone who knows her. I hope your country has sense enough to reward her in some way." He sat down at the table and accepted a cup of coffee but went on talking to Olivette. "I know more than most people about snitches and spies," he said. "Most of them work for money or to save their hides. She worked for her country. She must be the saint of spies, if there is such a thing."

He lit a cigarette and pulled an ashtray toward him. "I'm on my way to Munich," he said, "just came up from Garmisch, and I'll be going back down there right away. I need help in Garmisch." He paused and frowned. "No, I'll make that stronger. The *country* needs help there. I mean the USA, though God knows Germany needs help too. It's like the end of the world down there," he said, "as if no one ever heard of law or they think it's a joke. The regular townspeople live off the black market. They have to. I know we're supposed to give them fifteen hundred calories a day. Maybe we do, but what can you do but sleep on fifteen hundred calories a day? But it's not just the townspeople, it's all the outsiders, and all the loot and drugs they bring with them. It's as if we tipped Germany up on its south end and all the wreckage of the war slid down to Garmisch, like going into a funnel. There are still stray SS guys up in the hills like Indians in a western movie. There are DPs from the east, and Hungarians and Poles and Germans from the east all running from the Russians. There's no food except what the farmers are just starting to bring in from the fields, but the townspeople don't have any money, so they're buying potatoes and onions with their watches and jewels. But there's American and English money floating around, God knows from where, money to buy the looted stuff. I've even seen gold coins and old American bank notes. Like I say, it's the end of the world."

"Sounds like Sodom," West said.

"I'll tell you something else that makes me think of the end of the world," Delgado said, as if he hadn't heard West. "We've found people carrying radium cubes, practically glowing in the dark. Who knows where it came from? Hospitals in the east, I guess. And the Germans had an experimental atomic site up in the hills, all gone now, but we've heard rumors of uranium being moved. The town's practically a staging area for smugglers. Look at the map and you'll see that Garmisch is only a hop, skip and jump from Italy and Switzerland and southern France. We know all sorts of stuff is going out. We've stopped some of it—money going to Switzerland, artworks going to Italy, morphine and cocaine going everywhere—but it's like Chicago in Prohibition. You bust one outfit and while you're rounding them up three more go over the border."

West said, "What can we do to help you?"

"Give us expertise mostly, I guess," Delgado said. "We need to know the quality of some of that stuff being moved. We need to know whether it's the real thing, and where it came from, and where you guess it might be going." He stopped, cleared his throat, looked a bit shame faced. "My people are good cops, but they don't know Michelangelo from Mickey Mouse. Can't say I do myself."

West said, "We'll do what we can, but it sounds as if you need more than art experts."

"I know that," Delgado said. "I need the FBI and the Mounties and the Chicago police department, but I don't have them. So I'm doing what I can."

"We'll get our gear together and come down tomorrow," West said.

"Good," Delgado said. "I'll fix you up with the AMG people. Look me up when you get there. About what I've been telling you: I suppose you think I was exaggerating. I hope I was, but I don't really think so." He reached across the table and took Olivette's hand and held it for a moment. "It's been a real honor to meet you, Ma'am. When you see Madamoiselle Valland again, please tell her how much some of us honor her."

When he'd gone, Olivette said, "He was genuinely concerned, wasn't he? Not a cynic like so many policemen. He doesn't accept disorder."

"At least not total disorder," West said. "A policeman from Chicago must know you have to accept—"

"Yes, I know," Olivette broke in, "you have to accept the truth of imperfection."

I left them then, took the truck back to the motor pool to be gassed up, and got my blanket and mess gear. I took my carbine out of the cab and for the first time in a long while took it apart and cleaned it. I didn't think I'd need it, but it was in good order just in case Garmisch really was the end of the world.

Chapter 6

We got to Garmisch just before noon the next day. The road took us in a long slant upward to a gap in the mountains, and before we started on the down slope I stopped the truck, and we all sat and looked at Garmisch Partenkirchen. It looked like a painting, as if someone had been commissioned to paint the most beautiful place in the world and had done his best work. The valley was brilliant green, dotted with white houses with red roofs, and the white houses were dotted in turn with the crimson of carnations. It lay nested at the foot of mountains as if in a cradle, and a bright ribbon of water lay between the two towns. We were all thinking the same thoughts. Olivette, sitting as usual between me and West, leaned forward a little to get a better view. "If I were a painter," she said, "I would paint this place, and I would call it 'The Second Eden.'"

"Delgado says it has more than one snake, though," West said. "Maybe we'll find that out for ourselves."

We went down the long winding slope into Garmisch and found ourselves on the main street, the Bahnhofstrasse. Close up, the town looked as good as it had from up above. The war hadn't touched Garmisch physically, whatever it had done to its townspeople. Streets were neat and clean, shops seemed to be open, though of course we couldn't see whether they had anything much to sell. The American presence was everywhere: jeeps and command cars parked, GIs strolling the sidewalks, many of them with German girls. I almost expected to find a movie house showing American movies.

We stayed on the main street and came to the city hall, which was now AMG headquarters. It was a three-story stone building with AMG offices on the first two floors. The first floor had been partitioned into several cubicles. We heard typewriters clacking behind the walls. Two tech sergeants eyed us, then told us that Delgado's office was on the second floor. A corporal asked for our IDs, then took us into the office. It was a small room with windows overlooking the Bahnhofstrasse. It had been a civic office of some sort, because the desk and file cases were too ornate to be army issue. A picture of FDR was on the wall between the windows. Delgado got up from his desk to greet us, shook hands with West and Olivette and nodded at me.

"I figured you'd be here about now," he said, "and I skipped chow so I could treat you to a German meal down the street. You know, give you the feel of the place."

"Kind of you," West said. "Beautiful town you have here. We haven't seen any criminal types yet, though, just a lot of GIs."

Delgado said, without the hint of a smile, "Same thing in a lot of cases."

He told us he'd show us our quarters after lunch, so we left our gear in his office and followed him back downstairs and out to the street. "We'll go to the White Horse," he said. "Good food, all black market. Good beer—I think that's legit. And probably lots of criminal types too."

The White Horse Inn was about a hundred yards down from the city hall. It was a large, white two-story stone building with some sort of heraldic design painted on one side. The front door opened on the Bahnhofstrasse; the back side of the building was practically on the river bank. We walked into a large high-ceilinged room with enough wooden tables and chairs to seat maybe a hundred people. A bar with long-handled beer pulls ran along one side, and there was sawdust on the floor, damp here and there with spilled beer. Somewhere in back was a kitchen; we could smell boiled cabbage and sausage. Several of the tables were full, mostly with GIs. Delgado led us to a table in a corner near the bar. A woman with reddish blond hair was behind the bar. She looked to be in her thirties. When she came around the bar to wait on our table I could see that she was well laced into her dirndl dress and showed a good deal of cleavage. All she had to do was walk from the bar to our table for you to know that whatever dealings you had with her would be touched with her sexuality, even if you only ordered a beer from her.

She greeted Delgado with a mock curtsy which showed a little more of her cleavage. "Major Delgado, what a delightful surprise! And you have brought friends! Even more delightful!" Her English sounded rehearsed to me, but maybe it was supposed to be that.

Delgado waved his hand, as if to brush aside social trivia, and said, "We would like your daily special, Frau Hausner, with beer all around. But nothing from the black market, Frau Hausner, only legitimate things."

She pretended shock, crossed her hands on her breast. "What a thing to say! You must be joking, Major Delgado." She touched him lightly on the shoulder, then turned to the rest of us. "The major does not smile much, but he makes many jokes."

When she had left the table Delgado said, "That is Frau Hausner, Zenta Hausner, to be precise. She owns this place. When you understand how that can be you'll know a lot about Garmisch."

A boy of about ten brought our drinks to the table, steins of amber-colored beer with a collar of foam. "I don't suppose Frau Hausner knows any more about National Socialism than a flea," Delgado said. "But we know she was tight with the Nazis during the war. In fact, she was the girlfriend of the Gauleiter of Bavaria. In short, she should be on our blacklist: unacceptable, not to be trusted, not to hold any position of influence."

"But she's not on the blacklist?" West said.

"Was, but is no longer," Delgado said. He drank some beer. "Because she's now the girlfriend of an important person. That important person happens to be an American. We have here a civilian internment center, which is a fancy name for a holding pen for Germans on the blacklist or for persons we're suspicious of. It's not a concentration camp. It's very humane, in fact. The American officer in charge of this center is a man named Burger. A captain in AMG, I'm sorry to say. He's cleared her."

"You know that for sure?" West said.

"For sure," Delgado said, "but we can't prove it because Burger's destroyed her records." He drank more beer. "We have a snitch in the center," he said. "He tells us what Burger's doing, but by then it's too late. And it isn't just Frau Hausner that he's helped. The AMG has certificates made out for Germans who've been cleared of any Nazi connections. The German name for these is *persilschein*, but the GIs call them Annie Oaklies. Burger gave one of these to Frau Hausner, but he's sold some to other people who shouldn't have got them. We know this from our snitch too."

The same boy brought our sausages and potatoes and another stein of beer for Delgado. When any of us happened to look over at the bar, Frau Hausner waved and smiled. Just as we were finishing, an American captain came in and went up to the bar. Delgado put his stein down. "That's him," he said, "that's Burger."

The three of us looked hard at Burger. He was a little under medium height, slender, thin faced, a fringe of goatee on his chin. He and Frau Hausner leaned against the bar from opposite sides so that their heads were close together. At one point he turned to look toward our table. "Doesn't look like much, does he?" Delgado said. "They say power is sexual though." When we got out on the street Delgado's mind was still on Burger. "I'd like to get him for what he's doing," he said, "because he makes all the rest of us look like fools. He's able to do what he does because we won the war. But he does other things too. We'll get him for something."

We got our gear from Delgado's office, and Delgado's corporal came with us to show us our quarters. There was a gasthaus just around the corner from the city hall that AMG had appropriated. It was a neat little place with six or seven separate rooms. The corporal was careful to point out West's room without any mention of Olivette, without in fact even looking in her direction. I suppose Delgado had primed him. Then he took me across the street to a larger gasthaus. It was for noncoms, he told me, but guests were permitted. That night, after a little more of Frau Hausner's beer, I dreamed that Olivette and West and I were driving through mountains and as we came around a curve we saw a building with a marquee on the front, like a movie theater, and the marquee said "The Garden of Eden." Olivette said, "I should probably paint that," but we didn't stop because we decided it wasn't real.

The next two days West and Olivette were busy examining art material that Delgado's people had confiscated. West told me in the evening that they had found silver plate, communion chalices, tapestries, statuary, golden stationery boxes, anything that could be carried to a truck. And paintings: a Fragonard, several Dutch miniatures, even a painting by the American Thomas Cole. "No more Raphaels, though," Olivette said.

I found out that an AMG corporal named Schuermann who worked on the first floor was from Grand Rapids, and we got chummy enough that we went to chow together at noon. He sat at a desk just inside the front door, and it was his job to screen the Germans who came in to make complaints about the Americans. He'd got the job mainly because he could speak German. I sat with him for a while on two days while West and Olivette were gone, shooting the breeze about Michigan and baseball and the war, how Greenberg had gone into the army but so many others hadn't. The St. Louis Browns, he told me, had a one-armed center fielder named Pete Gray, and we wondered how he could possibly bat.

The German complainants straggled in and Schuermann beckoned them over to his desk and interviewed them. They were mostly old. There weren't any young men around any more, and though I'd seen several young women in the White Horse and on the street, none of them came to make a complaint. Schuermann shrugged when I asked him about it. "Most of them have GI boy friends to complain to," he said, "and I guess the others are afraid of us." We laughed about some of the complaints, but not about others. An old man complained that some GIs had crapped on his doorstep the night before. An old lady complained that she had traded household goods to a GI for rations and he had cheated her. Schuermann asked her for details. Two silver candlesticks and a silver serving dish for two boxes of C-rations, but he had given her only one box, and the cigarettes had been taken out of that. She didn't know the GI's name but she could point him out, she said. Schuermann took her name, but we both knew there was nothing he could do. Even if AMG found the GI it would be her word against his.

"And there's so damned many of us I can't keep track of them," he said. The Fifth Army had taken over this zone from the Third Army, but there were still all kinds of people from the Third Army milling around. There were GIs passing through, on leave or just freewheeling from other towns. There were even people down from SHAEF in Frankfurt, important people with lots of staff, because a lot of people thought some of the bullion from the Reichsbank had been sent down here and buried. So Schuermann listened and jotted down notes when the German people complained, but he almost never took the complaint upstairs to Delgado. He apparently had a knack of forgetting the complaints as soon as the person left, or so I thought, because it seemed to me that if he let them accumulate in his mind they'd be too much for him. Two days of the complaints were more than enough for me. A man traded the family Bible for cigarettes, but the cigarettes were wet and wouldn't light. A woman had traded a handmade coverlet for a case of C-rations, but all the cans were crushed and the food was spoiled. Books traded for condensed milk. Brooches for K-rations.

Linens for gasoline. Schuermann was like a GI Dear Abby, except that he didn't give out advice, just an occasional mechanical word of sympathy. After two days of that I spent my free time sitting by the river, looking beyond Partenkirchen to the Zugspitze, clean and white and unimaginably high.

I was sitting there on our fourth day at Garmisch when West and Olivette came around the corner from the White Horse Inn and found me. They came down the bank and sat on the grass next to me. "We have news," Olivette said. "Major Delgado thinks he may be able to arrest that Captain Burger he told us about."

"And we get to be part of it," West added.

Some joke that Burger had made about pictures had given Delgado's spy the notion that Burger was dealing in looted art, and the spy had reported this to Delgado. That was all the spy could tell Delgado; he hadn't any evidence, and evidence was what Delgado needed. "Delgado needs someone to do something illegal," West said. "He needs someone who knows something about art to break into Burger's house and see if there really are any pictures there, and if there are, whether they're of any value. That's Plan A."

"But maybe he wouldn't hide them in his house," I said. "He could have them stashed anywhere."

"Right," West said, "that's why there's a Plan B."

"Plan B is more interesting," Olivette said, "it's so much like a spy movie. But you might not like it, Jimmy."

"Plan B is a sting operation," West said. "If we find there's nothing in Burger's house, then we entrap him."

"How?" I asked.

"We set up someone posing as a buyer of looted art and have him contact Burger, drop hints without saying anything direct. If Burger's innocent he'll walk away from our man. If he's got something to sell, he may bite. He takes our man to the pictures, or takes the pictures to our man and—presto—there are Delgado and the MPs waiting. Delgado doesn't get him for selling Annie Oaklies, but he puts him out of action for art theft and smuggling."

I thought about it for a moment. "I suppose it might work," I said, "if we were lucky. Where would you find this fake buyer?"

"I volunteered," Olivette said. "I thought it would be exciting. But the Major thinks it should be a military person. He thinks Burger would find a military man more believable—two of a kind, two military criminals. Besides, Burger saw me in the inn that night."

"Burger had seen me too, so both Olivette and I were out of it," West said.

"Then the Major thought of you, Jimmy," Olivette said.

I thought she was joking, of course, but then I looked at West and waited for him to say, Yes, it was a joke, but he didn't. Instead, he said, "Here's the Major's thinking, Jimmy. He needs a stranger, someone Burger doesn't know, and he wants the stranger to be military. Burger knows everyone around town here, at least by face. He doesn't know you, and you're military."

"But he saw me too," I said. I felt like an anonymous man in a theater, sitting safely in the dark, who suddenly has a spotlight turned on him.

"He saw a GI sitting with Delgado and another officer and an attractive woman," West said, "from across the room. No offense, Jimmy, but he had only a quick look and you weren't the one he'd concentrate on. Besides, Delgado's idea is to make you a chicken colonel. Burger saw a GI, a cent a million, in dirty fatigues. He'll see a young spic and span colonel of combat engineers when he sees you again."

I knew they were watching my face to see my reaction. I tried to keep my face expressionless, because I wasn't really sure of what I felt. "This cloak and dagger business," I said, "this is all Delgado's idea?"

"Yes, he sprang it on us," West said.

"Well, what do you think of it?" I asked him.

Olivette spoke before he could reply. "At first I thought it would be a lark, playing a trick on a very bad man. That's why I volunteered. Now I'm not so sure."

West looked at her. "Why not? I mean, why not if Jimmy agreed?"

"Because it may be a nice trick," she said, "but it's a trick on a man who has a gun. If he sees through the trick—" She didn't finish.

"I suppose Delgado would say his people would be on hand," West said, "but I see your point. Something might go wrong. I don't think we were thinking about that when we volunteered ourselves."

We were all silent for a few moments. Then I said, "So you're not asking me to do this?"

West said, "That's right," and Olivette said, "No, we're not."

"All right, I'll do it," I said. I wanted to do what they had volunteered to do. It was as simple as that. "It may be my only chance to be a colonel," I said. I knew that was bravado as I said it, something out of a movie, but I hoped they didn't know that, didn't know how badly I wanted Plan A to succeed.

We met with Delgado late that night in his office; we had to wait till dark, and the spring days were getting longer. After my talk with West and Olivette at the riverside I had gone to my quarters in the gasthaus and stayed there till chow because we had agreed that I should stay out of sight as much as possible in case we had to use Plan B. Olivette had found a pair of outsized dark glasses somewhere, the kind people use after eye surgery, and I was to wear them whenever I had to be outside in the daytime.

This time when we went to Delgado's office he greeted me personally and shook my hand. I had the impression that he was seeing me for the first time, and I thought West had probably been right when he said Burger probably hadn't really seen me in the White Horse. I'd always suspected that officers saw GIs only in the aggregate, but I'd never had such clear proof. "I hope we don't have to use you, but I appreciate your volunteering," he said.

I only said, "Thank you, sir."

He had a large scale map of the Garmisch area spread out on his desk. "I'll show you where Burger's place is in a minute," he said, "but first I want us all to be clear on what we're doing." We pulled chairs over in front of his desk and he stood, half leaning, against the desk and looked down at us, like a teacher settling himself before a small group of students.

"We—or you, rather—are going to do something that is probably illegal. I say 'probably' because I don't really know to what extent a soldier gives up his constitutional rights when he's in the army. Maybe he still has protection against unreasonable search and seizure. I'm assuming that we have reasonable cause to think—or hope—Burger has stolen material hidden in his house. If we—you—get caught breaking in, I can't say what a military lawyer would do to us. I would certainly say I ordered the break-in, but that might not be enough to save you." He turned to Olivette. "As for you, Ma'am, since you're a French national I suppose you'd be turned over to French authorities, wherever they might be." He paused, folded his arms. "Now that the formalities are out of the way, we can get down to logistics. Gather round."

We all crowded around the desk and looked down at the map. "Burger's taken over a farmhouse about two miles out of town," Delgado said. He pointed to an X just off a thin line marking a secondary road. "There are some out buildings of some sort—a barn and maybe a chicken coop or something, but no animals. I suppose it's possible he's hidden things in one of those places, but I doubt it. They'd be damp and dirty, not the place for valuable paintings, if he has any. They're in the house, I'm guessing, or they're not on the farm at all. In that case we go to Plan B and our ersatz colonel." He nodded at me. "No offense, colonel. So it's the house we concentrate on. My snitch has been out there a few times. He tells me it's fairly big—six or seven rooms, at least three of them bedrooms. Fireplace in the living room, and no central heating, so maybe electric heaters here and there. There's a bathroom—tub and sink—but no toilet. There's an outhouse in back. It should be easy enough to get into the place, but I don't want evidence of entry in case we don't find anything. Of course, if we find something, then it won't matter. I've got a bunch of master keys which may or may not work on the doors, but no burglar tools. You'll have to improvise."

"When do we go?" West asked. "And how do we know when he won't be there? And does anyone live with him?"

"We know there's a big shindig tomorrow night at the White Horse," Delgado said. "My man says Burger's sure to be there. So we go tomorrow night. He has a live-in girlfriend, but we assume she'll be with him at the party. I figure you should have about two hours to work with. You'll have to wait till after dark—say nine to eleven."

"What if we find things?" Olivette asked. "What do we do with them?"

"Nothing," Delgado said. "I'll be down the road about a quarter mile with a couple of my men. We'll be out of sight from the road, but we'll be able to see the farmhouse. If you find something you turn on some lights, blink them a couple of times."

"One if by land, two if by sea," West said.

"Whatever," Delgado said. "Now look at the map. Get oriented."

We all stared at the map, and West traced our route with his finger.

"How do we go?" West asked. "Not in our two-and-a-half, I suppose."

"Jeep," Delgado said. "I guess the colonel can drive a jeep?"

I said I could.

"Then good luck," Delgado said. "Pick up the jeep here after dark and go do it. Bring me that bastard's hide."

The next day was very long for me. I kept to my quarters most of the time, but I hadn't anything to read except the French art book that Olivette had given me, and I found it hard to stay with that. I went to chow early because it was always most crowded then. Officers ate in a separate room, and I sat with my back to that doorway. Finally, late in the afternoon I put on my dark glasses, pulled my helmet liner low over my face, and took a walk along the river. Movement helped me to stop thinking about that night, but as soon as I stopped and sat down my mind went back to it. I saw the map again, spread out on Delgado's desk, the X marking Burger's farmhouse. I could see farmhouses from where I sat—solid looking buildings of whitewashed stone with red slate roofs—and I supposed Burger's place would look like them. They looked pleasant and unthreatening in the sunlight. But I'd learned something about houses at night. Even the ones you know very well seem different at night, and the ones you don't know are like strangers you bump into in a dark place when you thought you were alone. So I walked, and went to early chow again, and then at dusk I went to West's room, and the three of us waited for the dark. We had flashlights and a couple of screwdrivers, and West had a Swiss army knife with a dozen different blades and gadgets on it. Olivette had a nail file and some hairpins. If those things didn't get us into the house, we had no backup plan except to look for an unlocked window. We got into the jeep, Olivette sitting next to me and West crowded into the rear seat. We drove quickly out of town, then slowed down. We'd estimated that the secondary road we wanted was about a half mile out of town. The night was cloudy, but there was a half moon, enough light to spot the road. We followed it for another half mile. West had been peering over my shoulder at the odometer and checking it against his watch. He said, "This should be it," and I stopped the jeep. We sat and looked away from the road and toward where the house should be, and finally Olivette said, "I see it." I had been driving with just cats' eyes, but now I turned the lights off completely. When we looked toward the house, then back to where we were, we could make out a kind of lane, really only imbedded tire tracks, heading toward the house. I inched the jeep along for maybe thirty yards, till we could see the house quite plainly. Then I stopped and we got out and walked as softly as we could toward the house, no one in the lead, walking almost arm in arm.

There were no lights in the house. As we got closer I could see that it was much like the ones I'd seen in the afternoon, except that in the dark it seemed bigger. "Might as well try the door first," West said, so we went up to it, and when we were close enough to touch it I turned on a flashlight with a handkerchief over it to dim it and we looked at the lock. West got his Swiss army knife out and poked at it a few times. "Looks pretty formidable," he said.

Then Olivette said, "Turn the knob and at the same time put your blade in the crack—see if there is a—a—"

"Dead bolt," I said.

"Yes, dead bolt."

"Righto," West said. He turned the knob, slid the blade of the knife into the crack. The door swung open a few inches. We all stared at it. "It wasn't locked," West said. "Captain Burger has great faith in his fellow men. Or there's nothing in the house worth stealing."

"Maybe he is just absent minded," Olivette said. Finding the door unlocked had upset all our preconceptions, I suppose; we had geared ourselves to pick locks or climb through second-floor windows, and now all we had to do was walk through a doorway. So we did that, each carrying a flashlight, West pointing his straight ahead, Olivette and I pointing ours to the sides. I shut the door behind us and we advanced slowly into the front room. Our lights showed a fireplace on the left wall, a staircase on the right wall, a sofa and two chairs in between, an archway straight ahead into a dining room with a massive round table and several chairs and an equally massive buffet and china cabinet. We went slowly through both rooms and into a kitchen in the back. No pictures anywhere. I wanted very badly to see pictures. I pointed my torch in any corner or wall recess I could see, including the privy, opened kitchen cabinets full of pots and pans, examined a closet with a broom and mop and pail, even opened the oven door of the stove. I assumed that pictures would be stacked together somewhere, the way I had seen them at Altaussee, but when we found nothing I began to shine my torch over every inch of wall in the three rooms, because it occurred to me that they might be hidden in plain view, like the purloined letter in the Poe story, that they might be hanging on Burger's walls like family portraits. But there were only two pictures, a painting of the Zugspitze in the front room and a painting of the Virgin in the dining room that even I could see wasn't valuable.

We went slowly back to the front of the house, looking everything over a second time, trying to see things from a different angle, but there was nothing suspicious to see—no armoirs, no window seats, no desks with deep drawers that might hold rolled up canvases. We were talking in whispers, even though we were sure the house was empty, part of our identity as burglars, I suppose, and when we had looked the front room over again, West whispered, "The stairs," and we went over and started up, West ahead, me in the rear. There was a door at the top of the stairs and, to the left, two more doors. "Three bedrooms side by side," West whispered.

The door to the room at the head of the stairs was ajar, and West gently pushed it open and stepped inside. We followed the beam of his light and went in after him. The three lights showed a small bedroom with a narrow single bed, a small dresser at its foot, and a closet just inside the bedroom door. Olivette and I trained our lights on the closet door while West opened it. We heard him say "Ah!" and then "Come and look!" The three of us jammed together between the closet door and the bedroom door and looked as West touched the several canvases that leaned together against the closet wall. I let Olivette past me so that she and West could look at the pictures together, flipping them apart like pages in a book. West said, "Murillo," and a moment later Olivette said, "Watteau," and West said, "Another Rubens." I didn't try to look at the pictures. I leaned against the wall and thanked God instead. West said, "They look like the real thing," and Olivette said, "Yes, they do," but I didn't care whether they were real or fakes; they were loot, they were contraband, Burger was a thief, and now there would be no Plan B.

"Come look, Jimmy," Olivette said. They brought them out of the closet and leaned them against the bed, five of them. West pointed out which was which, but I couldn't really focus on them. The Rubens seemed to be all chubby angels, I remember, and the Murillo was a somber looking Virgin. Olivette said, "We should look at the other two rooms. There may be more." So we left the paintings leaning against the bed and went to the second bedroom.

The door was closed. West opened it, went in with me on his heels. I saw his light beam go up, then level, then abruptly down, and he said hoarsely, "Don't come in, Olivette!" But it was too late; she'd come in almost beside me. She didn't say anything; none of us did. The three flashlight beams stayed on the bed; then Olivette's went out. Burger was on the bed, on his back, naked, and obviously dead. His chest looked as if it had been spray painted with blood, and the blood beneath him had soaked into the sheets. His head was tilted back on the pillow so that his goatee pointed upward. His eyes were open, but his face showed nothing—not surprise or fear or pain, though, I thought, he must have felt all those things at his last moment.

"Let's go down and turn on lights for Delgado," West said. "We don't have to hurry away now."

We went down, found the light switches in the front room, and turned on what lights there were—a lamp near the front window and a lamp by the fireplace. I opened the front door to let the light be seen better, and then we all sat down and waited for Delgado. All our minds were on what we'd seen, but in different ways.

"Two houses and two dead men," Olivette said. "But we had nothing to do with this one."

"That's why the front door wasn't locked," I said. "Whoever did it went out that way."

"And it wasn't done for the pictures," West said, "unless whoever did it didn't know about them."

After that we were silent until Delgado and his men came. Two jeeps drove almost to the front door and a moment later Delgado and two MP sergeants came in and stood in front of us.

"You three don't look so good," Delgado said. "What's going on? Why all the lights?"

"Burger's upstairs dead," West said. "We found paintings in a different room. You'd better go up and see for yourselves. We didn't touch anything but the paintings. He must have been dead when we got here, but we didn't know that."

Delgado looked hard at West, then at Olivette and me. "That's it? That's all you know?"

"All we know," West said.

Delgado turned and headed for the stairs, with two of the MPs after him. In a moment we could hear their footsteps over our heads. One of the MPs came down, went to the front door, and called out to the one MP who hadn't come in to radio for an ambulance. Ten minutes later Delgado came back down. We were sitting side by side on the big leather sofa, and he pulled a chair over and sat down in front of us.

"We're not big crime scene people," he said. "We don't have the equipment. We don't even have a medical examiner to look at the body. But it looks pretty clear cut. We figure the girlfriend did it, unless he was entertaining men friends naked. We'll find her. Her clothes—or at least some woman's clothes—are in the bedroom closet, and the GIs at the internment center probably know her. She shot him five times. At least there are five rounds missing from the magazine.

"You found a gun?" West asked.

"Right beside the bed. His web belt and holster are on a chair in the corner. She shot him with his own gun. A Luger."

"Luger's a German gun," West said.

"Yeah, prime trophy gun," Delgado said. "He'd been carrying it. The holster was on his web belt."

Olivette said, "A German woman shot him with a German gun? Do you know why?"

Delgado seemed to search for words. "Well, Ma'am, everything considered—I mean lack of clothes and all—I'd say it was a sex thing. What's your French term for it? A crime of passion?"

"Yes, a crime of passion, no doubt," Olivette said, "but it would be interesting to know whether the crime occurred before or after the passion. It's possible she was defending herself against an attempted rape or some other violence."

Delgado seemed too surprised to answer for a moment. Then he said, "Well, unless she tells us we won't ever know, because we don't have the forensic medical people here to do an examination. I see your point, though," he said, and he really did seem to be considering what she had said. "I suppose you think we might pin it on her without a fair trial, sort of frontier justice."

"I don't defend her," Olivette said. "I only say that if she shot him you should try to find out why. You shouldn't treat her the way the Gestapo would treat a French woman in Paris."

"I take your point, Ma'am, I really do take your point," Delgado said. "I have to tell you, though, that since I'm the one in charge of this whole thing, my instinct is not to try too hard to be Sherlock Holmes. I have to find this girl, of course, and I have to hear what she has to say. If she denies shooting him, I can't do much about it. There's the gun, and there may be fingerprints on it, but we don't have facilities here to do fingerprint analysis. I may just let frontier justice take its natural course. A bad man—more to the point, a bad soldier—has been killed. I'm not sorry about that. And someone else can write his wife with the news."

"I didn't mean to compare you to the Gestapo," Olivette said. "That was only rhetoric."

"No offense taken, Ma'am," Delgado said.

By then the ambulance had pulled up to the front door. Two medics carried a folded stretcher upstairs. Quite a long time later they carried it down. They must have stripped the bed because on top of the body bag was a heap of stained bed clothes.

"We haven't talked about the paintings," West said to Delgado. "They should be packed up and moved before someone else steals them."

"Where should they go?" Delgado asked. "I mean, where does all the looted stuff get taken?"

"Right now, Munich," West said. "That's the collecting point for this area."

"Well," Delgado said, "how about if you take them off my hands? How about you take them to Munich?"

So we agreed to come back in the morning and pack the paintings and head for Munich. Delgado would post a guard on the house for the rest of the night. We were leaving for our jeep when Delgado stopped us just outside the front door. "Soldier," he said to me, "you won't get to make colonel now. I suppose you're disappointed."

It was the closest he came to making a joke. I said, "No, sir, but I'd rather make it the hard way anyway." That was *my* joke, and he actually laughed.

The next morning Delgado rounded up two GIs and two Polish DPs who had some carpenter skills to help pack the paintings. Somewhere they found some scraps of plywood and one-inch wide sticks and took them out to Burger's farm. I had already taken West and Olivette there, and I was getting my truck ready for the loading—cleaning the deck, putting the hoops up for the canvas in case it rained. I joined the carpenter party, and with a lot of improvisation we managed to set up a framework on the truck bed something like a bookcase turned on its side. It would let the paintings stand up in separate sections, and the framework was tied to the sides of the truck to prevent any movement. The five paintings, all padded with bed clothes and GI blankets, were slid into their places, I rolled the canvas down, and we were ready to go. We said so long to the GIs and the DPs and headed out of town for Munich. West had said he saw no reason to talk to Delgado again, and I think both West and Olivette felt as I did: that Garmisch was perhaps the most beautiful place in the world, and that we were glad to leave it. We never heard how Delgado handled the murder investigation; he'd said it would be like frontier justice, which probably meant short and perfunctory. He was a Chicago policeman, and Chicago policemen hadn't bothered their heads when Capone's mob and rival mobs killed each other off.

The road to Munich was clear, and we were in Munich by early afternoon. West knew where the collecting point was: a building that had been a Nazi party headquarters in the center of town. Munich had taken a lot of bombing. Near the city center many of the main buildings were still draped in green fishnet camouflage covers, but Munich was in much better shape than places like Mannheim that had been shelled to pieces. The collecting point was on a broad street called the Koenigplatz. It was a massive building, the roof still partly damaged from bombing, with MPs at the main entrance. West showed his credentials and went in, and in a few minutes he came back out with another lieutenant and two POWs. They unloaded the paintings and carried them inside. By the time he came out again it was late afternoon, and West decided it was too late to start back for Neckarsulm.

"We can bunk in here for the night," he said. "Our paintings will pay our room and board. How about a little side trip? Why don't we grab a cup of coffee here and ride over to Dachau? It's only up the road."

Chapter 7

We'd heard a lot about Dachau in the last few days, from Armed Forces Radio and *Stars and Stripes,* and what we'd heard sounded unbelievable. We knew it was a German concentration camp—that was the term everyone was using—and that Seventh Army guys had gone in and liberated the prisoners. But from what we heard it wasn't a camp like the one I'd seen when I drove the French prisoners back toward France. We'd heard stories of bodies stacked up like firewood and gas chambers and cremation ovens and medical experiments, things that sounded like stories out of hell. We didn't know what to believe, and we didn't know what we'd find when we got there, but we decided to go.

Dachau is—or was then—a pretty Bavarian town, really a suburb of Munich, and the camp was on the town outskirts. From what we could see from the street, it was a broad sprawling place fenced in by a ten-foot high brick wall as far as we could see. There were several high iron gates set in the wall, and we stopped at what was clearly the main gate, guarded by MPs. We could see a knot of people inside the gate, some in civilian clothes, some in uniform. They were standing in a semicircle, apparently listening to a man in civilian khakis standing in the center. Next to him was something that looked from our distance like a larger than usual golf cart carrying two large humped objects covered with a tarpaulin. West got out and went up to one of the MPs at the gate. Olivette and I sat in the truck staring at the iron lettering woven into the bars high up on the gate: *Arbeit Macht Frei*—work leads to freedom. Olivette said, "The Germans have a strange sense of humor, don't they?"

West came back to the truck. "Those people inside are from the States. They're making a documentary film about the camp. The GIs in there are from the outfit that liberated the camp, the 45th Division. There are cameras on that wagon. The idea is to go through parts of the place and stop here and there and film while one of the GIs talks about what he saw there and did there. We can go along if we don't get in the way. The MP says it'd be a shame if we missed the place. He says everyone should see it. The whole world."

So I parked the truck and we went through the gate and stood on the edge of the circle. The man in the center was finishing up his talk to the group. His khaki shirt and trousers gave him a kind of military look, but he wore a baseball cap with a New York Yankee logo. "We want it quiet as we move," he said, "because you won't know when the sound is on or off, and we don't want to have to cut out a lot of crap later on." He pointed to the cart. "There'll be a man on each of those cameras all the time, sometimes filming, sometimes not. When we stop somewhere I'll say a word or two for the camera, and then our GI heroes will take over. And just a word to those GIs: we don't expect you to be orators; we just want you to tell the camera the way it was." Two men also in khakis climbed onto the cart and pulled off the tarp, and the speaker—I supposed he was the director—got in a tiny front seat and started the electric motor. A lieutenant wearing the 45th Division's Thunderbird patch walked beside him.

We followed along. "Heroes?" Olivette said. "Of course they may be heroes, but to call them that to their faces! How *gauche*!"

"How Hollywood, you mean," West said, "or how New York."

After about fifty yards we passed a long one-story building and came to the start of a barbed wire fence probably fifteen feet high. It ran parallel to the brick wall, about thirty feet inside it, and inside the wire fence was a ditch about five feet deep that paralleled the fence. Fifty yards further back were the first rows of battered buildings that we knew had been barracks. The scene explained itself. No one coming out of the barracks could escape unless he went through, or over, the ditch, scaled the barbed wire fence (which was electrified and would kill him), and climbed the outside brick wall before the guards in the watch towers shot him dead.

Our procession stopped at a place along the wire fence that the lieutenant had pointed out. The director, the lieutenant, and three GIs huddled for a few minutes next to the cart. Then the director pointed to one of the GIs and said, "Okay, you can get us started. Take your time. When I say 'Go,' just start telling what you saw." One of the cameramen pointed his camera at the wall, and the GI went over and stood by the wall, looked up at it, then turned back toward the camera, ran his tongue along his lip and started to speak. I felt for him; you could almost smell his nervousness. But when he'd talked for only a minute I knew it wasn't just stage fright that bothered him. It was what he'd seen. He couldn't find words to say what he saw because what he saw was beyond words. Years later, when I ran across Homer's description of Hades, where the smoky shades of the dead ran toward Tiresias, begging for blood, I remembered the private from the 45th Division who'd tried to tell what he saw.

"I was in I company," he said, "we came over the wall about here 'cause the gate was locked, and the Germans were shooting at us from the towers, and we shot back and killed them all." Then he looked through the wire fence, he said, and that was when he saw them for the first time. They were coming out of the barracks in waves, he said; it was like a wave of striped suits coming at him and he thought they were dead, their bones all sticking through the suits, and they poured into the ditch and out of it and up to the wire fence, and there was this sound they made, it was almost like a chant, he said; they were all saying the same thing but he didn't know what it was. He was scared, he said; he didn't want them to touch him. Someone must have turned off the power, he said, because they came up to the fence and put their bony arms through it and held them out to him and made that sound. And then, he said, all of a sudden he realized who they were, and some German soldiers came along holding their hands up, wanting to surrender, but he shot them. Afterward he found out they weren't guards; they were combat troops who'd been in a hospital there, but he almost didn't care, he said, though he was beginning to care now, beginning to feel bad about it.

The director said "Hold it!" to the cameramen. The GI didn't seem to hear him. He had paused, but now he started to speak again. The director said, "No, that's enough, soldier," and one of the other GIs went up to him and half led him back to the group.

"He was crying," Olivette said. "I wonder if they will show that part."

We were moving slowly past a long low rectangular building that looked like some sort of storehouse. One of the shorter walls was heavily pockmarked. Another one of the GIs pointed to the wall, and though the director hadn't called for a stop we stopped anyway because it was clear that the GI wanted to say something. "They were lined up against that wall," he said, "must have been a hundred of them. They had their hands up in the air or behind their heads. We were just standing there watching them. Then a guy opened up with a machine gun. I didn't even see him at first, then I saw the Krauts falling over on top of each other, and I looked around. He was crouched behind the gun blasting away. A colonel came running over and kicked him away from the gun. I don't know how many he got, thirty or forty I guess." The lieutenant said, "Maybe not that many. There was a lot of confusion, a lot of shooting."

"It was the corpses," another GI said. "The fucking corpses were everywhere. Some of them piled up like firewood, stiff as boards. Someone said there was a boxcar full of them outside the camp. It was so wild, so wild. They didn't look real, nothing looked real, not even the Germans when we shot them."

The last stop the group made was at the crematoriums. There was an old one and a new larger one. They looked like pizza ovens except that the openings were larger and rounded. Someone said they could handle two or three corpses at a time. There had been corpses there, too, the lieutenant said, when they'd first got there. The Germans had run out of coal for the fires and hadn't had time to drag the corpses up the hill and bury them, so there were the corpses piled like trash. "We went into town," the lieutenant said, "and we rounded up all the civilians we could find and we brought them out here and made them help us with the burials. I suppose that violated the Geneva Convention, but no one thought of that at the time. We wanted them to see, and we wanted them to smell, because we knew they'd all say they hadn't known what was going on here, and we knew they'd get away with it, but at least we could make them do the burying. I suppose they could have refused, but it's just as well they didn't. Our guys were pretty much on edge that day."

We went back out the main gate and to the truck. It was late afternoon now, the sun low, the camp behind us sliding into shadow bit by bit. "You were right," West said to the MP who'd let us in. "Everyone should see it."

"But everyone won't," the MP said.

We drove back to Munich in silence. We hadn't made any real provisions for staying that night, but luckily the MFAA people at the Collecting Point said we could bed down in some of the unused offices on the second floor, maybe even some place close to where Hitler had sat with the party bigwigs and discussed the ways to make Dachau more efficient. So we made do with some warmed over C-rations, and then an

MFAA corporal showed us our quarters. It was dark by then, and he led us up to the second floor with the help of a flashlight and a Coleman lantern because there was no power on the second floor. In one good-sized office they had put two cots for West and Olivette, and in a smaller room two doors down they had put a cot for me. Forty feet down the corridor, they told us, were a sink and a flush toilet that actually worked.

The corporal said, "The lieutenant apologizes for the lack of power, but it can't be helped. He said he offered some things as compensation." He laid several fat German candles on the enormous desk that sat almost in the middle of the room, and then reached into a musette bag and brought out two very large bottles of wine, put them on the desk next to the candles, and added three small squat glasses that might have been jelly glasses. "Rhine wine is the house wine at the moment. The lieutenant hopes you like it." He lighted one of the candles and set it on the desk in a dish made out of the cover of a C-ration can and wished us goodnight.

"You'd better take one of these, Jimmy," West said and handed me one of the candles. "When you get settled come on back and we'll try some of the Rhine wine."

I lit the candle and took it down to my cubicle and shut the door behind me. I hadn't ever bedded down so close to Olivette and West in our travels; it was almost as if we had adjoining rooms in a hotel. There was a smaller desk in my place and I found a piece of ceiling tile for a base and put the candle on the desk. I put my blankets on the cot and sat down. I was tired from driving, and more than tired from Dachau. The camp we had seen was dirty and depressing, but at least it had been empty. I recalled some of the pictures we'd seen in *Stars and Stripes* of the stacked corpses, and now I had seen some of the places where the stacks had been. I could have been one of those Thunderbird GIs that had gone over the wall and seen what they had seen. I'd been through infantry basic in Benning, and people just like me had gone to divisions like the 45th. Some whimsical army directive had sent a few of us to the engineers instead. I couldn't imagine myself shooting German soldiers trying to surrender, but probably the GI who'd told us about it couldn't imagine himself doing that either. What he'd seen had changed him. I supposed it would have changed me, but I would never know that.

There was a light tap on my door, and West pushed it open and said, "The table has been set and the party's about to begin." I snuffed my candle and followed him back to their office.

They had lit two more candles, and the three were spaced close together in the middle of the desk like a candelabrum. Three battered metal chairs were clustered at one end of the desk, a few feet apart. The two bottles of wine stood at that end of the desk next to the three glasses. West poured wine, and we sat down, Olivette between West and me. Without preamble we talked about Dachau. It would have seemed wrong not to.

Olivette said, "We were like detectives at the scene of a crime, after the crime is over. I can't help thinking what it must have been like to be there when it all happened."

"I was thinking that too," I said. "I could have been there but for luck." I told them about my infantry training.

"I'm glad you were not there, Jimmy," Olivette said. "I would not want to see you like that young man who cried."

A surge of warmth ran through me at what she'd said, and I thought I could feel myself blushing. I thought of trying to make a joke of it, but it was too important to me, and so I said nothing.

West sipped his wine and looked off into space the way he did when he was thinking about something, but he didn't say anything. After a moment or two Olivette said, "It's difficult not to think about the grand questions, isn't it, when you've seen Dachau, and when you can imagine what was done there?"

"Grand questions?" West said.

"Evil," Olivette said. "If what was done there is not evil, then the word has no meaning."

"Yes, it was evil, God knows, no dispute there," West said.

"'God knows,'" Olivette echoed him. "That's just the problem, isn't it? I mean, if you believe in God. He knew, but he didn't do anything to stop it or prevent it." She looked at me. "I don't mean to insult your religion, Jimmy. I was Catholic as a child. I suppose most French people were. We learned that God is all powerful and also that he loves us, and even died for us. We believed we had individual guardian angels watching over us. But there were no guardian angels at Dachau, were there?"

I didn't answer. I knew she didn't mean to hurt me. And what she said about Dachau was what I felt too. I'd been a Catholic child too, but I wondered now if I could still believe like that child. It's so hard not to imitate people whom you admire, so hard not to try to think as they think.

She said, "I don't see how after Dachau anyone can believe in a loving God. Maybe if one has led an ordinary life—has worked and gone to church and got married and had children—and has never seen any evil except perhaps an illness or a death in the family—then perhaps one could believe in that God and be comforted in that belief. But no, not after Dachau. After Dachau that belief seems to me willful blindness, an obscene stupidity."

"Whatever brute and blackguard made the world," West said.

We both looked at him for explanation. "It's from Housman," he said, "not a great poet, but he said a few things perfectly. 'Brute' and 'blackguard' are what we might call God after Dachau if we insist on thinking of Him as a kind and loving father God. And we surely have more right to complain than Housman."

I didn't say anything. Then West stood up, reached for the bottle and poured more wine. I stared at the lighted candles on the desk. There was no draft in the room; they burned straight upward, like the candles at mass. We had learned all the Latin terms for the things involved with the mass—the paten, the chasuble, the censer, the cruets. I hadn't ever been an altar boy, but I still remembered the Latin responses at the mass, *mea culpa* while the bells rang, *domine non sum dignus* when taking the wafer. It all seemed worlds away from Dachau, and from what Olivette had said about God. I looked at West, willing him to say something to mitigate what Olivette had said.

"When we talk about God we should remember St. Paul," West said. "When we're children we think as children, see through a glass darkly, and so on. God the loving father, God the omnipotent creator. Dachau wipes those notions out, we think. Those are children's notions. But we shouldn't be children now, should we?"

"Exactly," Olivette said. "We're adults who see that there's nothing to believe, nothing out there, or up there. Just ourselves."

"Yes, just ourselves," West said. "And when you know what people like ourselves did at Dachau it's hard to say much for us. But as Jimmy pointed out back at Hitler's house, we're not all like Hitler. We didn't murder and cremate people at Dachau, although we might have, I suppose, if we were in the same circumstances as the murderers—born with their minds, raised as they were raised, open to Nazi thought as they were open. But what can we say about ourselves that's positive? Years ago, I saw a movie, a documentary about some forlorn place in Africa, and one image from the film has stayed in my mind. An old black man in rags was standing in front of his house, a hut of straw and twigs, and he had a twig broom in his hands and was tidying up the dust in front of the hut. I felt pity for that man. I knew that his misery was wrong and could be remedied. I felt that, and I felt that at Dachau, and I know that you did too. We can love, and pity, and help—but we're not omnipotent. We're not God—not the children's God, at least—but we have in us something that hates evil and wills good to other people. We call it being humane, but it may as well be called charity."

Olivette and I looked hard at him, expecting him to go on, but he didn't. Finally Olivette said, "That's God, then? That's God, this charity that not all of us have?"

"I'd say, that not all of us have all the time," West said. "I imagine that the SS troops at Dachau had their moments of charity, that at some points in their lives they had done good things for others, had pitied and loved others."

"Your democracy of the imperfect again," Olivette said, "making us all alike."

"You remember we agreed that all soldiers loot," West said, "German, French, American. I don't defend the SS. I only say we're more alike than different, and that we have the possibility of being better than we are, or of being better more often than we usually are. That's all we can point to. That's as far as we can see now. Like St. Paul."

"I like the old God better," Olivette said, "even though I don't believe in him. At least I could blame him for Dachau."

"You can still blame him," West said, "just keep it in the family."

We talked some more about Dachau after that, but no more about God. One of the things that Olivette found so awful was the fact that most of the corpses burnt up in the crematoriums or buried up on the hillside were nameless. "Not people," she said, "just lumps of flesh dumped in a ditch. I suppose we can hope that the Germans kept records of all of them, so that years from now people can say that their loved ones died at a certain place, like saying that one died at the Somme. But if you died at the Somme you were called a hero, weren't you? What can you call someone who died at Dachau? A victim?" Her voice broke, and I could see that West had leaned toward her and taken her hand. "*Merde, merde.*" Her voice was forced and uneven. "*Merde, merde*, everything is *merde*, war is *merde*, and Dachau is the worst *merde* of all."

She stood up and brushed the tears with her fingers the way women do, as if they're angry about crying, and when I turned to leave she and West were standing together and he was smoothing her hair and saying something very quietly to her. Maybe he was simply saying, "There, there," as you do when a child is crying. If so, it was as good as anything else, I thought, because nothing you said about Dachau could be comforting.

I took one of the candles off the desk and went out and visited the toilet that really flushed and then went to my room. I got undressed and sat on the cot and stared at the candle. The Rhine wine replayed for me West's words about God and Olivette's tears about Dachau. I had certainly felt anguish and pity about what had happened at Dachau; I certainly wished I could have helped in some way. But my feelings were not special; everyone would feel as I did. Except of course the people responsible for Dachau. But even they, West said, had the capacity for pity and love, though that capacity hadn't been used at Dachau. Everyone, then, all of us, were capable of charity. And that capability was divine, was God—more evident in saints than in others, but present in all of us. So God wasn't to be blamed for letting Dachau happen, because he wasn't omnipotent and omniscient; he was the charity that all of us possessed in some degree, and should possess in a greater degree. Dachau happened because we weren't as charitable as we should be—not full enough of the divine pity. Years later, in philosophy classes, I would learn about the emergent God and the process God, I would read Hegel and Whitehead, and I would argue about God's immanence and transcendence. But that night in Munich, staring at my candle, my mind muzzy with wine, I had never heard of those things. I only knew that if West's God depended on people like me, on our capacity for charity, it seemed to me it wasn't a presence at all, only an idea. And I was like

Olivette. I wanted a person, even if only a person to blame. I blew out my candle and lay down on the cot, and after a while I went to sleep. I dreamed I was in a zoo, and all the animals threw themselves against the bars of their cages and called to me, and I was immensely sorry for them.

Chapter 8

Next morning we had breakfast with "the antiquities people," as the MFAA section was called, begged some bread and cheese from their mess hall, and left for Neckarsulm. It was a beautiful early fall morning, and as the road turned here and there we could see the mountains we were leaving behind shimmering in the morning sun. We got behind a GI convoy going into Augsburg and lost time, but by just past noon we were outside of Stuttgart, and we stopped and ate our bread and cheese and finished the wine from the night before. "We could be posing for a Monet," Olivette said, "'*Picnic on the Grass Near Stuttgart*.'"

West said, "Better add 'during wartime,' considering how we're dressed." We looked at each other and began to laugh. West and I were in faded and grimy fatigues, and Olivette was still in her unique uniform of Ike jacket and nondescript blue men's trousers. "We need a picture of this," Olivette said, "because when we tell people about us years from now they won't believe us."

Remarkably, when we pulled into the motor pool in Neckarsulm, a lieutenant from AMG was showing off a Leica that he'd got in some way he didn't specify, and he was taking pictures of everyone he could find. "God must have heard you, Olivette," West said. The lieutenant posed us sitting on the front bumper of my truck, with Olivette between West and me.

As we were leaving, Olivette said, "I never noticed the name on your truck till now, Jimmy." She pointed to the Hankus-Pankus name stenciled across the hood. "Is that like hanky-panky? I know what that means."

I laughed, and so did West, but he didn't know what it meant either. "It's a nickname for Hank Greenberg," I said. "The radio announcer always called him that. He was a hero of mine."

West explained that Hank Greenberg was a baseball player in Detroit.

"He's playing baseball during the war?" Olivette said.

"No, he's in the army somewhere," I said. "That's one of the reasons he's a hero."

She touched West with her left hand and me with her right as we walked out the gate. "I have my heroes too," she said, "even though they're not well known and even though I don't say that to their faces."

Neither West nor I said anything, but I wondered if he was as pleased as I was.

In the days that followed it seemed to me that the picture-taking lieutenant was just one example of the wartime mentality changing over to the occupation mentality. He wasn't the only one looking to take home, or send home, souvenirs. Combat units were being rotated back to the States and replaced by service units and late draftees. When you went into the PX now you didn't hear much war talk—who'd been where in the Ardennes fight, or what the Germans had done at Bitche. Now it was talk of what these new people were going to do, where they'd get to go on leave—maybe Paris or Brussels—whether the PX beer would ever improve, where to find the easiest German girls.

And something else happened that told us the war was really over and the civilians were taking over. When I remembered it years later I thought of it as "the Wiesbaden thing." Someone high up in the chain of command had got together with people high up in the civilian world of the States, and they had decided it would be a good thing if a lot of great paintings from various German museums should be sent to the States for viewing. These were paintings that had been stored for safety in various places like Altaussee, but they weren't stolen. They belonged to Germany. They'd been picked up by the Monuments people along with looted things and brought to different collecting points. The people who had this idea argued that these paintings would be safer in the States—in the National Gallery in Washington, for example—than they would be in German museums that had been partly destroyed or that couldn't be maintained because of shortages of coal and electricity. The pictures would eventually be returned to Germany, these people said, though they were vague about a date. Some of them even suggested that Germany didn't deserve to get them back at all, though, as West explained, that was a minority view.

The MFAA people were outraged. West said, "We're probably going to prosecute the ERR people for stealing French and Dutch art and telling everyone it was just for safe keeping. And then we're going to do much the same thing? If the Germans don't hate us for being conquerors, they'll hate us for being hypocrites." There were meetings that West had to attend, in Munich and Marberg, where he and the other antiquities people planned strategy for preventing the whole thing. We heard that some of them tried to resign their commissions or refused to have any part of selecting the pictures or packing them for shipment. "It's ugly," West said. "The worst of it is that we can't make the other side understand how wrong it is. We tell them they're acting like conquerors, but they don't care because they *are* conquerors. *Vae victis*. We may have to do something really drastic."

The thing went back and forth all through October, and then the MFAA people got lucky, or they thought they did. A magazine writer from New York got wind of the plan and made it public in the States. "That's what we need," West said. "When it gets out in the open I think American public opinion will sink it." He was wrong, though. Either the public didn't get enough of the story, or it didn't care, or maybe it agreed with the plan. Anyway, the fight was over. "We'll follow orders because we're soldiers," West said, "but we'll do it under protest, public protest." They did. They got together and wrote a protest paper and sent it off to the press. West showed me a copy. They appealed to a higher law than that of the army, they said, and argued that to commandeer "the heritage of any nation" was no more than pillaging and theft. They sent it off, and that was the inglorious end of the matter. About two-hundred pictures were taken, packed, and shipped by boat to the States. "We fought the good fight," West said. He'd had something like sympathy for Herr Granz and even for Hitler, but he was simply angry at the people who wanted to take the paintings. I thought Olivette might see the irony of this, but she was as angry as he was. The papers picked up the story, and the protest paper was called "the Wiesbaden Manifesto," after the name of the collecting point that the pictures were taken from. West told Olivette and me that several of the MFAA people had resigned their commissions and gone home.

"I'll do that too, pretty soon," he said. "But there's one more thing I want to do as a Monuments officer."

"It's an important thing," Olivette said, "maybe something that will partly make up for this stupid theft."

The important thing was a ceremony to be held in Paris to celebrate Rose Valland's work at the *Jeu des Paumes.* "I do not know if it is an official ceremony," Olivette said. "Our government is a shambles at the moment. But many people who know the worth of what she did will be there. There will be speeches, I suppose, but probably not a medal. Alan and I want to be there."

"And the only way I can get there is by being a Monuments officer," West said. "That title's losing value pretty fast at the moment, but I think it'll get us to Paris and back. After that, we'll do what we have to do."

We were sitting at West's kitchen table drinking powdered coffee. I looked at them as they talked so casually about going to Paris. Paris, Rose Valland, the *Jeu des Paumes*. I had gone past a Parisian suburb in a forty-and-eight and had found poetry in the name on a sign post. To go to Paris now, to see the little lady who had fooled the Gestapo, just to be able to say, "Yes, I was in Paris after the war, it was everything they say it is—the Seine, the Louvre, the sidewalk cafes—too bad you couldn't have been there." I knew my time with West and Olivette had to end soon, but to see Paris and Rose Valland with them would somehow validate that time, would end it in a moment of shared glory. I was sure now they would ask me to go with them, and they did.

"Talk to your CO," West said. "See if he'll let you go. I'll put in a word for you if that'll do any good."

I had a moment of sheer joy at the invitation, so intense that I was able to believe for that moment that I could actually go. But as I headed for the orderly room to see my CO I could feel the elation dying into simple hope. It was too good to be true. I knew that. It would have been wonderful. I knew that. It wasn't going to happen. I knew that too, somehow, knew I had run out of luck. When the CO said, "You've been on the gravy train long enough, soldier," I wasn't surprised. I felt the same way. When he said, "You pull your details here, not in Paris," I was silent. I couldn't have given him a single reason why I should go except to say that I wanted to so badly.

I didn't even get to drive West and Olivette to the airfield at Stuttgart because some field grade officers from AMG were going to Paris too, and they were all riding together in command cars. So I said goodbye the night before they left. We had a glass of wine in the kitchen and

I wished them a good trip. "We'll be back in a week at most," Olivette said. "So not 'goodbye,' just '*a bientot*,' Jimmy."

West shook my hand and said, "Keep the faith, Jimmy." I said I would, though I knew it was just a phrase, like '*a bientot*.'

They may have come back in a week. I never knew. Two days after they'd left, our AMG section got word they were going to Japan. I had a choice. I could go with them, or I could go to an embarkation point and be discharged, because I had enough points to get out. But if I did that I'd be shipped home. It wasn't a real choice for me, of course. I couldn't imagine going to Japan. I didn't even want to be discharged—at least not just yet. I wanted to see what West and Olivette were going to do when they got back. So I said I'd take my discharge. I'd hoped to slow things down and kill time till they came back, but once I'd made my decision it was all out of my hands. The most I could do was go to West's apartment and leave a note, and then I was in a hurry and couldn't decide what to say. Finally I told them what had happened and said I hoped we could get in touch somehow. But I felt odd saying that. We had been good companions in arms, even friends, but I knew they were far more important to me than I was to them. We had shared Altaussee and Berchtesgaden; we'd watched Herr Granz's painting disappear in flakes of ash; we'd broken and entered a house and found a corpse there; we'd seen Dachau, in fact and in imagination. But we had never traded the small intimacies of our lives. They knew I was from Michigan, but I didn't know where West came from, or whether Olivette was really Parisian. I laid her French art book on the kitchen table with a note stuck in like a bookmark. I didn't trust myself to say anything in French, and I couldn't think of anything in English that wouldn't be mawkish, so I simply wrote, "Thanks for the book and for everything else. Jimmy." On another piece of paper I wrote my home address and left it next to the book with a glass as a paperweight. But as I left, I knew it wouldn't do any good, even if they came back and found the note and the book. We'd been together over there in a way we never could be anywhere else or at any other time. We had been wartime friends, and now the war was over.

Chapter 9

I waited three days after Catherine Dunne had phoned I called her in California. At the end of the third day I had no more idea of what to say to her than I had when she phoned me. I had promised to think about her father, and I had done that now, as well as I could, but now I was supposed to report to her on my findings, and I couldn't say what I had found. Or rather, I couldn't say anything of value to her. I could tell her a good deal about myself at nineteen, but she wasn't interested in me. Of course, I could tell her that for months after I had come home I had hoped to hear from her father, even though I knew I'd never see him or Olivette again. Even a token note to say Olivette had got her book, or Rose Valland had had her celebration. Not anything that would extend the friendship—I was sure that was over—just a courtesy note, a note to say goodbye. But nothing came, and after a while I began to explain the failure in different ways. Even if they had come back to Neckarsulm they might not have found the notes. Units were coming and going those days. There must have been a lot of confusion. New officers might have taken over West's apartment, and the notes might have been lost or misplaced or just thrown away. And then I thought, too, that there had been two or three GIs in my original company that I'd exchanged addresses with, but we'd never written to each other. It didn't mean that we hadn't been friends; it didn't mean anything at all.

So finally I had stopped thinking about West and Olivette except when there was an occasional story in the news about GI thefts of artworks in Europe, or the problem of tracing the owners of looted paintings. They reminded me of what West had said about the coming black market in stolen art. And there was the story, too, of the looted gold train and the rumors that there were still millions of dollars of gold bullion hidden away in the Bavarian mountains. They had even made a movie about that. I always looked hard for any mention of a Raphael painting of a young man, the one stolen from Poland, any suggestion that it still existed, and especially any suggestion that it had somehow been destroyed. But there was no word of it. West had said we'd never know what Herr Granz had burned that day, and he was right. But after a few years, like most other GIs, I pretty well forgot the war and the looting. After all, I hadn't come back shell shocked or crippled. I'd merely been away for three years. When the stories broke about the looting of the national museum in Baghdad I read them with little more than a layman's interest and a citizen's indignation that our military people in Iraq had been stupid or careless enough to allow great parts of the museum's treasures to be simply carted off. I wondered, too, if later stories would tell us that American troops had joined in the looting, if there had been more Captain Burgers in this newer war. But I didn't look for such stories; the American looters would just be faceless GIs for me, and the looted treasures would not be things I had seen and touched.

But the trouble with these remembrances was that they were not useful. They were mostly about me, not West. Catherine Dunne's father figured in them, of course. I could say, I wish your father had written me a note sixty years ago. But I didn't really believe that that failure was a matter of character. I could find excuses for that. So when I picked up the phone to call his daughter I had no clear and distinct message for her, only a clot of memories that were mostly about myself. At the last second, while her phone was still ringing, I grabbed a strategy from somewhere. I would tell her that I would write her a letter, that my thoughts were too jumbled to tell over the phone. It was a transparent evasion, of course, and she saw through it immediately.

"I'll tell you what, Mr. Adair," she said, "I've put you to a lot of trouble, and I won't put you to the extra trouble of writing a letter. I'll fly in and we can have a talk." I started to protest, because a talk was the last thing I wanted, but I hadn't an alternate suggestion at hand and so could only say the usual banalities—don't want you to take the trouble, too expensive, lost time, and so on. "I have nothing but time," she said, "and I love to fly. Besides, I want to meet you. And I found a few things in my dad's papers that I think you'll be interested in."

So that was that. I guiltily offered to meet her plane and to put her up at my house, but she had her own plan. I thought later that she probably had intended to come to Michigan no matter what I said to her. She asked for the name of a motel near my house that had limousine service with the airport, and when she had that information she said, "Fine, Mr. Adair. I'll fly out and phone you from the motel, and we can talk whenever it's convenient for you."

I couldn't say there was no convenient time for me, of course, though that was so—no convenient time to talk about memories muddled by time and about the gaucheries of sixty years before. I waited for her phone call next day like a student dreading an oral exam he's not ready for.

She must have taken an early morning flight, because she called about two in the afternoon. She was at the motel. I could come over whenever I liked. I couldn't imagine that a delay would make things any easier, so I said I'd come over at once. The motel had a small patio behind the main building with a few umbrella tables set out. You could bring drinks out from the bar inside if you liked. She was at one of the tables, a carafe and two cups and a brown envelope in front of her. I stepped out onto the patio and stopped, and we looked at each other for a moment, putting faces to the telephone voices from yesterday. When she was sure it was me she stood up and came over to me. She was tall, like her father, but that was the only resemblance I could see.

"Mr. Adair?" she said, and held out her hand.

I shook her hand and said, "Yes. I hope you had a good flight."

"Oh, it was fine," she said. She gestured toward the table. "I ordered some coffee for us. Or we could have a drink if you like."

We both sat down. "Coffee's fine," I said. She was wearing white slacks and a black and red blouse with a kerchief at her neck, and I thought anyone would know she was from California. Something in the way that Californians dress and seem to feel so at home outdoors says they're not from cold northern places. In the shade of the umbrella her face was only faintly lined, although I knew she must be in her sixties.

"I know I'm imposing," she said, "but it's only for a little while." She poured coffee for me. "I forgot to ask for cream and sugar," she said. "I can ask for some."

"Black is fine," I said, "and you're not imposing on me. I'm only uncomfortable because I think you want more information than I can give you."

She didn't look like her father, but I thought I saw some hint of him in the way she turned away, then back to me, and smiled. She hadn't seen very much of her father and yet she had taken on one of his mannerisms. Would similar personalities show themselves in outward signs? Nature or nurture?

"Maybe you think I'm snooping," she said, "but honestly I'm not snooping for dirt or scandal. My dad's dead, and years ago my mother buried anything he did over there that she didn't like. That's if she ever knew about anything. They got divorced. Maybe there was enough fault to go around for both of them. I think there usually is, but I don't care about that. I just want to know what he was like." She took a sip of coffee. "On the plane I was thinking about this—this digging into the past. You know how orphans sometimes want to find their real parents, not to blame them but just to find out their medical histories? To find out if diabetes runs in the family or something like that? Well, I'm my father's daughter, and my mother's daughter too, and I think I know what I take from my mother, and I want to know what I take from him. Does that make sense to you?"

I said, "Yes. I mean, I can see what you mean, but I don't know that it makes genetic sense. You inherit something of his genes, but you saw so little of him that it's hard to believe you picked up anything from his behavior. And we generally inherit both ways, inside and out." I knew I only half believed what I was saying, that I was only talking because I was uncomfortable.

"Well, anyway, I just wanted to say I'm not going to judge what he did over there. I assume he was unfaithful to my mother. In his notes and diaries there's an ON whose name keeps coming up, and ON is obviously a woman. ON and Jimmy—that's you. Those names, over and over. ON and Jimmy and I went to somewhere or other, and ON and Jimmy and I did this and that. I thought, If I could find ON and Jimmy I'd probably find out a lot about my dad. So I went looking for you two." Here she stopped and opened the envelope lying on the table. She slid a small snapshot out of it and laid it on the table in front of me. "ON and Jimmy," she said.

It was the picture of West and Olivette and me sitting on the bumper of my truck, the Hankus-Pankus visible on the hood behind Olivette's head. My heart began to thump hard and I caught my breath. West must have gotten back from Paris or he couldn't have had the picture. That was all I could think for a moment. They'd come back and probably found my note, but West hadn't written, even to say goodbye. All my rationalizations disappeared, and I was as torn for a moment as I had been sixty years before.

"She doesn't look especially pretty," Catherine Dunne said.

"She was, though," I said, "she really was. But she was more than pretty."

Catherine Dunne turned the snap over. Something had been printed in pencil in small, uneven block letters on the back. The letters had faded, and I held the snap out in the sunlight for a moment. The printing said: "GOLDEN FRIENDS." The letters and the quotation marks were spidery and thin. I turned my head away and stared out into sunlight, afraid of showing tears. I didn't need a goodbye note any more. The two words weren't ones anyone would write when he first saw the picture; they were words written some time later, looking back. And the printing showed something more about that later time.

"It isn't dated," Catherine said, "but it was in with some other notes and letters that he must have put together. Some of them had names underlined or circled with a red marking pen. I think I know why." I waited, but I thought I knew what she'd say. "I think it was when his mind was going," she said, "and he knew it and was trying to stop it." She was able to keep her voice steady, but she couldn't hold back the tears. She reached into her purse for tissue and dabbed at her eyes. I leaned across the table and touched her hand. She looked at me and tried to smile. "We're crying together, aren't we? Do you need a tissue?"

We didn't talk for a while after that. Two gulls from the lake landed on the patio and pecked at things we couldn't see. The silence was companionable. We'd become closer to each other. She looked at the picture again, turned it over and looked at the words again. She said, "There are quotation marks around the words, as if they were taken from something. I called a literary friend of mine last night and asked him if he recognized 'golden friends.' At first he said he did, that they were from Shakespeare: 'Golden lads and girls all must/Like chimney sweepers come to dust.' But that didn't seem right. It was 'golden friends,' not 'lads.'"

I suppose because I saw West's words as so wistful and elegiac that it hadn't occurred to me that other people might not see them the same way. "They're a Housman poem," I said. "Your father once said Housman said a few things perfectly. He must have thought this was one of them."

With rue my heart is laden
For golden friends I had,
For many a rose-lipt maiden
And many a lightfoot lad.

She listened carefully, repeated a line or two. "Old age and death, isn't it? Is that the end?"

"No. Four more lines," I said.

By brooks too broad for leaping
The lightfoot lads are laid.
The rose-lipt girls are sleeping
In fields where roses fade.

She said in a choked voice, "I'll always think of those words when I think of him, whether they're the right ones or not. And I suppose I'll always cry then too."

After a while she said, "I'm mourning him more now than I did when he died. I was really alone there at the funeral. Now I see he meant something to you too."

"I'm glad I didn't see him at the end," I said. "Maybe it would have been better if you hadn't either." Then, because her tears had made me more willing to speak of West, I said, "You want to know what he was like. Well, he was the kindest person I ever knew."

She looked at me as if the word was strange to her. "Kindest?"

"Kindest," I said, "most charitable, least wanting to hurt other people. Someone defined a gentleman as someone who never inflicts pain. He was like that."

She thought about that for a moment. "I guess I shouldn't be surprised. He was always good to me, the little I saw him. Maybe I thought that's what fathers were supposed to be. You associate kindness with women, though, don't you—I mean usually. Talking of inheritance, I have to say my mother wasn't especially kind. I take after her in that, maybe. Pushy."

A moment before she had been crying, and she looked as if she might cry again. "You're too hard on yourself," I said, "maybe harder than you are on your father."

She looked down at the other picture on the table, then pushed it over to me. It was a black and white snapshot of a gravestone—no real background, just a blur of gray that might have been sky or grass or just blur. The picture had been taken close up so that the lettering on the stone was legible.

Olivette Marnier Normandin
L 'Epouse/La Mere/La Patriote
1910-1972

I turned the picture over, but there was nothing on the back. "Was this in with the other picture?"

"No. It was in his billfold. Along with a picture of me when I was about seven." She paused. "It made me wonder if that was the only picture of me he had. Maybe it was. At least I didn't find any others in his things. Maybe I never sent any others. I don't remember one way or the other. It makes me seem cold, doesn't it?"

"You didn't make the situation," I said. "You didn't send him away. If anyone was at fault it wasn't you."

She said, "Thanks. I tell myself that, but sometimes it seems like an easy way out."

I thought I understood what she was doing: blaming herself so that I wouldn't blame her. We all have to save face, and I was the only person in the world who might have cause to blame her.

"I was thinking about dates," I said, "Olivette's dates."

"I've been through all that," she said. "He came home early in 1946. As far as I know he never went back, at least not to stay. My mother would have known about that."

"Maybe he went back when she died," I said. "Maybe someone wrote him. Or maybe someone sent him the picture."

"Maybe anything, I suppose," she said. "But I know he didn't go back to be with her. In a way I wish he had."

I thought I knew what she meant, but I said, "Why?"

"Because it would mean he loved her," she said.

"*L'epouse* and *La mere,*" I said. "She may have already had a child."

"So did my father. Me."

"Maybe that's why they both went back home," I said.

"Maybe anything again," she said. She pushed her cup back and forth in her saucer, frowning. "I have to ask this," she said. "Was he in love with her when you knew him?"

For a moment I forgot she was West's daughter and that she'd been crying and that I meant to be careful with her. I looked down again at the motorpool snapshot, at the three faces smiling into the camera, and I said, "I believe they were in love with each other. I believe that as much as I believe anything."

"Then I wish it had turned out better," she said. "I suppose that makes me a romantic."

"Maybe," I said, but the words "turned out better" had no meaning for me. For sixty years I had believed, and would always believe, that over there, in that time, what Olivette and West had had was simply good. And I realized now that the more Catherine and I talked the further we were from understanding each other. She was outside; she was looking at a slice of history; she needed to know dates and places. But when she had all the dates and places she still wouldn't know what she wanted to know about her father. I had been inside, but what I wanted to tell her about her father were things that I could hardly put into words for myself.

"I told you your father was kind," I said. "I'll try to tell you what I mean by that."

"I'm listening," she said, "believe me, I'm listening." With her elbows propped on the table and her chin in her hands, she waited.

And so, hunting for words, I began. I tried to explain that the end of the war was like the end of the world and the start of hell, something out of the *Book of Revelations*. Fires still burning from the bombing. Famine. Pestilence—typhus among the DPs, syphilis among the troops. But the worst thing: no innocence except maybe in the children begging for food. Everyone stole, or looted, or raped, or lied for food, or turned their neighbors in as Nazis. French, German, American—it made no difference—there was no innocence, only shades of sin. No platform of goodness to stand on and look down on evil. We were all on the same level. War obliterates goodness, I told her, and we had all been in the war. "And for all these people," I told West's daughter, "your father had pity, found partial excuses for their actions, put himself in their places and sympathized. He even excused God for allowing Dachau. When everyone else hated, he refused to hate. I say again, he was the kindest person I ever knew."

Catherine Dunne hadn't moved while listening to my catalogue of horrors. Now she sat back in her chair and said, "You make him seem like Jesus. Do you mean that?"

"No, I don't," I said, "and I think he would have laughed at the notion. I think he simply had more imagination than most of us have, and that he found it easier than we do to put himself in other people's shoes. That's surely a basis for love, isn't it?"

"I suppose it is," she said.

"We saw that in him," I said. "We didn't talk about it, or put a name to it the way I've done here."

"But ON saw more than that," she said.

"Yes."

She stood up and held out her hand. "Thank you, Mr. Adair. I think much better of my father than I did. No, that's not what I mean. I mean I think he must have been remarkable, and I'd never thought of that before."

I watched her walk away. What I had told her about her father was true and important, I thought. In a way I had redeemed both West and Olivette for her. And after sixty years it was a lift of spirit to know that West had thought our time together as golden. My own debt to him, and to Olivette, I hadn't mentioned to his daughter. I had tried to picture for her the chaos of our world after the war by calling it apocalyptic and conjuring up Durer's Four Horsemen. What I hadn't said was that in that swamp of meaningless cruelty and maniacal hatred—Herr Granz burning the picture, the stacked corpses at Dachau, the sacked rooms of the Eagle's Nest—West and Olivette had led me to solid ground. They didn't mean to teach me, and they didn't; they simply went their way, talking of Rose Valland and Rembrandt and Leonardo and color and perspective, and I began by envying them, then imitating them, then finally on some low level thinking like them. On the surface, Germany was the apocalypse, but underneath, in the salt mines, were the hidden treasures, the order and structure and meaning abandoned above. In the dim light of Altaussee I had put aside the war and even put aside the need to be like West and Olivette. It was said of the Knights of the Grail that in following the Grail they took on some of its attributes; they "partook of the

Grail," they caught a glimpse of the substance underlying all the accidents of time and change. I thought of the Hemingway story about the soldier in the Great War whose wife had died. He was angry, he said, because he couldn't stop grieving. He was angry, he told Nick Adams, because he hadn't found something that could not be lost. But West and Olivette had found that something, and had helped me find it. I had no better word for it than Keats' word, when he looked at the unchanging nature of the urn and called it beauty.

About the Author

A native Detroiter, R. J. Reilly graduated from high school in 1943 and, following basic training, was assigned to a U.S. Army Combat Engineering battalion that saw service in France and Germany during World War Two. Discharged in 1946, like millions of other veterans, he went to college on the GI Bill. He received MA and PhD degrees in English and American literature and began a university teaching career that lasted until his retirement in 1987.

After retirement Reilly's attention turned from scholarly writing to fiction. His four novels and two volumes of short fiction include *Over There* and *Weekend in the Country*, novels that draw on his experiences during World War Two. *The Pelican Affair* is set in Oxford, where Reilly taught a summer course at Corpus Christi College. *The Bronte House* and the short story collections deal with people caught up in problems of love and marriage and, occasionally, those of religion and philosophy. Reilly has said that he writes for "literate adults, people for whom fiction is storytelling that portrays the complexities of human existence."

If you enjoy Reilly's fiction, you may want to read his scholarly works: "Henry James and the Morality of Fiction," winner of the Norman Foerster award for the best scholarly essay in *American Literature* in 1967, and *Romantic Religion: A Study of Owen Barfield, C.S. Lewis, Charles Williams, and J.R.R. Tolkien*, published in 1971 and reprinted as an e-book in 2006.

Reilly welcomes your comments at rreilly16@comcast.net.

CPSIA information can be obtained
at www.ICGtesting.com
Printed in the USA
FFOW01n1415280715
15501FF